THE SEABRIGHT SHADOWS

Elizabeth, bound to a marriage she wants no part in, is strong willed and determined to free herself from the arrangement her father Silas has made. But she is trapped. The family's fortunes are linked to and dependent upon her marriage to Mr Timothy Granger, a man she despises. It takes a bold act of courage and the interference of her Aunt Jessica to make her see the future in a different light and save the family from ruin.

VALERIE HOLMES

THE SEABRIGHT SHADOWS

Complete and Unabridged

LINFORD
Leicester

First published in Great Britain in 2008

First Linford Edition
published 2008

British Library CIP Data

Holmes, Valerie
    The seabright shadows.—Large print ed.—
Linford romance library
    1. Love stories
    2. Large type books
    I. Title
    823.9′2 [F]

    ISBN 978–1–84782–263–5

Published by
F. A. Thorpe (Publishing)
Anstey, Leicestershire

Set by Words & Graphics Ltd.
Anstey, Leicestershire
Printed and bound in Great Britain by
T. J. International Ltd., Padstow, Cornwall

This book is printed on acid-free paper

1

Elizabeth stood at the entrance of Marshend Manor. Dressed in her warm riding outfit she breathed deeply, refreshing herself with the cool salty air. She loved rising early and feeling the wind on her face as she rode along the flat sandy beach that marked the boundary at the northern edge of the estate and the unruly sea beyond.

She stared ahead of her, along the avenue of trees that sheltered visitors from the strong north easterlies. Elizabeth was looking towards the estate gates when a movement distracted her, followed shortly by the distant sound of horses' hooves striking the hard surface of the newly laid drive. She stopped on the top stone step in mid descent and watched as the carriage entered the drive to the grounds. She recognised it instantly, her heart saddened and as the now familiar anger returned, she spontaneously clenched her fists. 'Damnation, not now!' Elizabeth exclaimed, then added in a quieter voice, 'Not ever!'

She walked slowly backwards towards the security of the large black doors. Although she knew this moment was coming, Elizabeth had hoped the man inside would not arrive for another few days, or a week at least. She needed time to collect her thoughts. Precious time, whilst she mulled over her father's words to her: 'You are too old to be gallivanting around the estate like a lost child'. His words had cut her soul like a knife, for she had never imagined he viewed her in such a manner. What he had told her next had frightened her with, what was to Elizabeth, their damning content: 'It is time you settled down to having your own children and looking after the needs of a good man. Elizabeth, you have been humoured for too long, you're forgetting your place in this world and it is unbecoming of a young maiden.'

Elizabeth had tried to make him see reason — her reason — for wanting to stay free. She had offered to help on the estate and build it up anew once he was too old to manage affairs on his own; neither point had met with anything other than derision, with no understanding from the man she had always loved and respected. Worse still, she had been dismissed, leaving him in a foul temper, and her bereft of the father she thought adored her. Meanwhile, their plans — his and those of her mother, Pollyanna — had been put into action.

This was to be the moment that she dreaded. This man's arrival heralded the forthcoming betrothal and, with him, her fate would be sealed. Elizabeth saw the carriage pass by the laburnum bushes nearer the manor house, their family crest clearly visible on the side and unmistakeable. 'Mister Granger!' she muttered acidly under her breath, as she stepped back into the shadows of the colonnades that framed the entrance to the building she loved as her home.

Elizabeth had no desire to be seen.

Her heart began to beat faster. Mr Granger was a senior partner of a firm of lawyers in York; a grave young man by what she had seen of him to date, which was not much. In his appearance he was dreary and dull. Her father had encouraged him and even helped the youth — now a man — in his career. The young woman could not understand her father's interest in him for he was indeed dour. Where he was concerned there appeared to be nothing humorous in life. He was always serious and the matter of her forthcoming engagement — a match made behind her back — was none of his business in her opinion but not, unfortunately, in the eyes of her parents. Where Mr Granger was, trouble for her usually followed close behind. He had the singular ability to put her father in the most serious of moods and her mother into a pensive state.

She ran straight down to the servants' passage, leading her to the kitchens at the back of the large manor house. The flagstone floor and bare stone walls emphasised the patter of her footsteps as she went.

'Miss Elizabeth!' Dora Root exclaimed disapprovingly. 'What on earth are you doing coming in here like this? Your mama would have you locked in your room for a week if she found you in the servants' quarters. You should know your place as we do ours!' The woman was shaking her head and her cloth cap flopped from left to right and back again in a state of confusion.

'Then do so, by being good enough as to not lecture me so, Dora!' Elizabeth snapped back sharply, but then looked down dejectedly.

Dora stared at Elizabeth's flustered figure, but then tilted the young woman's chin upwards and smiled comfortingly as she appeared disturbed by Elizabeth's distressed face, her manner softening. 'What is it, miss? What has got you in such a foul temper?'

'Dora . . . ' Elizabeth began, but

hesitated for a while as she looked at the ruddy cheeks of the woman she loved, who had helped to raise her from a baby, not caring how etiquette dictated she should treat her maidservant. 'Mr Granger is here! He may even have the old man with him whom I am expected to wed. I did not linger long and look for I could not bear to see whom I am being . . . ' she peered up at Dora's grey-blue eyes and searched in a most dramatic fashion, whilst feeling quite distraught, for an adequate word to express the desperation she was feeling inside, ' . . . sold to, for I know he will be hideous and I shall not go through with the wedding! They cannot make me.'

Dora looked at her and sighed deeply. 'Sold you call it! Miss Elizabeth, for shame on you . . . sold indeed. There's many a poor girl who would swap places with you, and you cannot compare your circumstance with the abomination of slavery.' The maid shrugged her shoulders at her as the mood did not lift. 'Oh dear, Miss Beth, how you take on so! It was bound to come to this at some point. You should be happy, for what young girl doesn't want to marry a wealthy man who can keep her in the style of life she has been brought up in . . . or a better one even.' Dora smiled at her, but even her best effort made no difference to her mood. Her mind was set.

'My lifestyle is the best it can be. I am happy. My mother and father both love me . . . or I thought they did until now.' Elizabeth looked sulkily down.

'Shame on you, miss, for they care more about you than anything on God's earth. To say such a thing is a sin.' She waved a stubby finger at her. 'Sit yourself down by the fire a moment whilst I finish off here and then I'll make you presentable. If we hurry we should be able to change you out of that riding outfit and into your best white muslin morning dress before anyone sees you.'

'Dora, I must talk with you most

urgently. When I saw Father this morning he said such strange things to me. He wants me to go away with this man. Why? If I am to be married then surely I should be sent for the Season to London first, should I not, and meet the best of the best?' Elizabeth grabbed her maid's hand preventing her from leaving her side. 'Mama met Papa there, so why should I not meet a young man of my own choice and fall in love like they did?'

'No, you should not.' Dora patted Elizabeth's hand. 'I'll be straight with you. Lass, they would poke fun at you because you were raised up here in the wilds — as they see it. You would be like a fish out of water and would be ill equipped to deal with their high-handed ways. I worked down there once, a long time ago, and believe me; I know what I tell you is the truth. Be happy and trust in your mother and father's preparations, for they know you better than you do yourself. At least be good enough to meet the man.' Dora was almost pleading with her. 'How do you know that you shall not fall in love with him in time?'

'I know it. It is one of Father's old cronies for sure; someone 'safe' who he knows, has known for years. He told me himself.' Elizabeth scowled.

'When did he tell you the man was old?' Dora asked.

'Did you not listen to what I said. I can read between the lines even if you can't.' Elizabeth was appalled when Dora laughed at her remark.

'Lass, you have no idea. You have a whole life before you to find out about your husband. Be patient.'

Dora smiled kindly enough at Elizabeth but it only riled her further, for now she, too, was treating her as immature and she was not and intended to show her . . . no, shock her, in order to prove it so. 'I shall have to pack some essentials and leave here, Dora. I shall go away and lead my own life.' Elizabeth watched Dora's face change expression as soon as she had spoken, her words having had the desired effect upon her maid.

Dora shook her head, frantic at the thought that her mistress would consider such a ruinous act. 'You'll do no such thing. No one would marry you if you did follow through on such a stupid notion. Honestly, Miss Elizabeth, I believe you would be naïve in the extreme to even try it. Headstrong and foolish! But I beg you not to even think upon it. I shall inform your papa of your intentions for your own safety if you suggest such an action again; you see if I don't.' Dora stormed off into the dairy, chuntering to herself, before returning a few moments later as Mrs Tuttle, the cook, appeared from the storerooms with a group of maids. She was exchanging orders and instructions with the kitchen hands regarding the household's meals. Mrs Tuttle was instantly flustered when she saw her young mistress sitting in her kitchen looking so concerned.

'No need to make a fuss, Mrs Tuttle,'

Dora said quickly, removing the look of concern from her friend's face. 'We're just leaving. Right, Miss Elizabeth, sorry to keep you a waiting here, I must have forgot me manners. Now let's be getting you all ready to greet your . . . 'guest'.' Dora held out her hand to Elizabeth, who realising her careless words could have been so easily overheard, if not for her maid's quick-thinking, took it gladly.

Elizabeth followed Dora's ample figure as she led the way across the vast kitchen and up the servants' staircase towards the upper landing.

'Did you hear what I said, Dora?' Elizabeth asked sharply.

'Yes, Miss Elizabeth, I did. You have to remember your father is a man moving on in years. Now, don't you be getting any notions of running off by your own self. Whatever would become of you, I shudder to think. It is a far different world out there, miss, than within the safety of the walls of this estate. Calm yourself down and we'll make you fit to greet Mr Granger.'

'Father is not old, Dora. He's strong and fit,' Elizabeth answered indignantly. 'Anyway, I should not worry about my meeting Mr Granger for he is just the messenger boy.'

Dora glanced back with a look of concern upon her face. 'I didn't say your father was old now, but we all age — there's no escaping that. Time and all . . . and your time to wed is here, so be gracious and honour your parents' wishes. Tell me, Miss Beth, did you really listen to what your father was trying to tell you or did you go off half-cocked?'

Dora replied sharply and with little sympathy, Elizabeth thought.

'I did! Well, I heard enough. The truth of it was obvious and I left when I could stomach no more. I wish he had not come, Dora. Do you think he is just visiting Father to see how he is? Perhaps my betrothed has decided to cast his net further south. If so, Mr Granger will not stay more than a few hours. Father might be able to convince him we will swiftly find a suitor for me more suitable and to my liking and then Mr Granger shall not stay at all. After all it is none of the man's concern, and besides which Father is always saying how time is precious, where business is concerned.' Elizabeth knew this was mere wishful thinking. Mr Granger never came unannounced or for casual visits. He always had a motive. Elizabeth's sense of foreboding over her father's precarious decision was intensifying as Mr Granger neared. Her father had spoken to her that very morning. He was agitated and very concerned about her response to the subject of matrimony. On his table lay a letter in Mr Granger's own hand. Her father was usually a man of good spirits, light of heart, but he had looked most troubled. He had told her of strange things, words that were frightening in their simplicity, yet their consequence was only just sinking in. That is why she had been taking the fresh air, thinking about her future, wondering if she dared to leave the estate on her own. She would need to take clothes and money, her horse, possibly . . . she had pondered if that would be stealing. Where would she go? It seemed a fanciful and far-fetched notion, yet possibly the only one open to her other than to comply with their wishes. Mr Granger's arrival had made everything more imminent.

Dora turned to face Elizabeth. She was watching her closely, yet she appeared to be lost in thought. 'What is it, Dora?' Elizabeth asked, as she took off her bonnet, flicking out her long dark hair.

'Oh, nothing, miss. Only I was just thinking how quickly time does go by. Where is that impish child I knew such a short time ago?' Dora sighed. 'And yet in some ways it appears a very long time since she climbed the estate trees and was for ever in trouble with her mama.'

Elizabeth noticed the serious tone

enter into Dora's voice and it gave her a moment's cause for concern. 'Have I changed that much?'

'Not really, and yet you are now a beautiful young woman, no matter how much of the child remains inside.' Dora patted her shoulder then added, 'Make sure you always keep a little of that child, Beth. It will make your life a happier place.'

'How do I do that?' Elizabeth persisted.

'By asking a whole lot of annoying questions for one.' Dora looked at her, shook her head and uttered a few kindly words. 'Intelligent, pretty and yet so naïve,' Dora added quietly.

'I don't want to see Mr Granger, Dora. He always upsets Mother in some way. Can't you say that I'm sickening for something?' Elizabeth looked hopefully at her maid knowing she would not; not even should she order her to. She may have felt lighter in spirit than a few moments before. However, it did not last long. As they reached the upstairs' hallway near the oak bedroom, their timing was such that her aunt was already walking across the main landing. She had wasted no time in readying herself for Granger's arrival. She almost seemed to be in a hurry to reach the main stairs, until their unexpected appearance interrupted her intentions. Jessica saw Elizabeth and Dora before they could return unnoticed to the kitchen.

'My dearest Elizabeth,' her narrow face broke into a tight-lipped smile, 'have you finally found your true place in this world?' Jessica, Elizabeth's aunt, added with a sarcastic smile growing on her sharp featured face. She was her father's sister and was accommodated at the manor at his insistence and on his charity.

'Good morning, Aunt,' Elizabeth said as calmly as she could, greeting her as if none of their previous conversation had happened, her face already quite flushed. 'I am surprised you are dressed so early in the day,' Elizabeth added as

16

her aunt was loath to rise before midday.

'You are in the wrong place, my dear. Tell me, Beth, should I inform your lovely mother as to where you wile away your empty hours?' She stared at her niece as Elizabeth paled at the thought.

She shook her head. 'That won't be necessary, Aunt, it is a rare enough occurrence.'

'I didn't think it would be, but you take silly risks for a young lady. You have to maintain standards in order to keep the servants' respect. Isn't that so, Dora?' She looked at the maid who blushed slightly.

'Yes, ma'am, it is so.'

'There you are. Make yourself presentable and do not slip down the servants' stairs again unless you wish to be schooled severely and arduously until you have studied and learned how a lady is expected to behave.' Jessica stared at a chastised Elizabeth. She looked along the corridor.

'We have a guest arriving today, do

we not? In fact, if we walk to the landing you might catch a glimpse of your intended.' She gestured to her niece to walk with her along the corridor towards the wide sweeping oak stairs.

'I should change first, Aunt Jessica.' Elizabeth took a step toward her bedchamber.

'Oh, don't be so grim, girl. You shall not be seen by him. We shall merely peek. Come!' She took Elizabeth by the hand and walked her to the upper landing. There standing against the wall, they could see the figure waiting in the entrance hall below.

Dora let out a long slow breath, and glanced nervously at Elizabeth, who shrugged her shoulders and stared blankly down at the man below.

Mr Granger was dressed, as was his custom, in black boots, fashionable straight trousers, and a fitted coat cut straight at the waist with long tails hanging behind him. The brilliant white of his shirt accentuated his dark hair, healthy complexion and tall frame. It had been some months since Elizabeth had seen him at Marshend and decided he had matured somewhat since she last paid him any attention. She glanced around him for any sign of her betrothed but was surprised by her own disappointment. No one was to be seen so she decided they must have made the messenger boy wait outside her father's office, whilst he greeted her intended.

Jessica stretched out a finger to flick one of Elizabeth's ebony locks away from her angry, flushed cheek. She seemed to enjoy taunting or belittling her.

Elizabeth pushed her hair behind her ears, annoyed with herself for letting her aunt find her in such a sorry state. Elizabeth noticed, but did not comment on Mr Granger's newly cut fashionably shorter hair. As a youth he had had hair that fell over his shoulder and tied at the nape of his neck.

'So what do you make of your

intended, child?' Jessica asked and looked at her curiously.

'Heaven's no, you are mistaken! That is Granger, from the legal firm Father has dealings with. He is not my intended.' Elizabeth spoke quietly but assuredly.

'Yes, I know who he is.' Her aunt looked at her, surprised. 'Your father is full of praise for the work he has done in building up his businesses. He is said to be a man who has foresight and will be excellent for the future of Marshend.'

'Well whatever he is, that is not the man I am to marry! He is just the messenger boy,' Elizabeth said tartly and was surprised to see her aunt almost flinch at her words.

'You are wrong, Beth. It is Mr Timothy Granger who is your intended. Are you not excited at the prospect at all, girl? Your fiancé will soon be introduced to you and no doubt all explained in full.' Jessica was looking at her carefully.

'No, you are wrong, Aunt. I have no wish to marry a man I have never met. I do not know his age, personality or disposition. He could be a rake and my life could be in ruins.' Elizabeth could see the growing confusion cross Jessica's face. Elizabeth was feeling less at ease and uncertain of her facts.

'Do you not trust my brother to have determined otherwise for you? Do you not think he would secure you a good match?' Jessica was smiling at her nervously in disbelief.

'Parents cannot always discern these things. On paper he may look one thing and in reality he could be the complete opposite. Yet here am I, supposed to just sit and nod and do his bidding. Well I shall not! Surely, you of all people should understand that!' She snapped the words out in no more than a whisper, but no sooner than they were released from her untamed mouth she had wished she had thought before speaking so forthright.

Her aunt paled, almost cringing at

her niece's outburst. She bodily straight-ened removing herself from being so close to Elizabeth. The thin lips pursed and she drew herself up to her full height before walking proudly past Elizabeth without looking back or offering a reply.

'Aunt Jessica, I'm so sorry . . . I didn't stop to think . . . I . . .'

Her aunt lifted her hand to silence her as she kept on walking. 'No matter, child, what is said cannot be with-drawn.' Her words drifted quietly in the air leaving an ice-cold silence behind them.

2

Elizabeth returned to where her maid waited patiently for her outside her bedchamber.

'Miss Elizabeth, that woman may annoy you, but she's lost everything through that drunkard and wastrel she was matched to. Don't you think your papa would give your future more attention than risking that for you?' Dora looked vexed. 'You don't know the half of it. Miss, you need to trust that Mr Seabright has, as always, your future happiness in his thoughts and control.'

Elizabeth knew she spoke the truth, yet she stared through her before entering her room. It was very out-spoken of her to be so direct. However, the one person who had always spoken openly with her was Dora. Elizabeth's own mother had been somewhat removed from her in her childhood, as Dora had seen to her every need from being a baby. Mother was someone to admire and respect and she knew that her father hoped that one day she would emulate her.

Before Dora could join her, another voice echoed down the hallway. 'Elizabeth! Elizabeth!'

The maid put her head around the door jamb to see the slight figure of Elizabeth's mother walking quickly toward her, her arms outstretched and her smile wide. 'Miss, you best greet your mama,' Dora said quickly as she ducked back out of the way.

Elizabeth made her way to the door and forced a smile upon her face.

'Oh, my dear child, I am so excited for you. Are you not happiness itself at the prospect of your future? Is it not just grand? He is here at last! So handsome a man, and soon . . . soon all shall be settled at last and we may rest easy once more.' She hugged her daughter to her. Then, almost immediately, she released her and stepped backwards into the corridor. 'No, Elizabeth, that will never do . . . you . . . your clothes . . . they smell of horses. Dora, send up hot water immediately. You will have to bathe her and dress her hair most fine for I shall not have him thinking you are of no, or little, culture. Elizabeth, you shall be like a princess today. My daughter will be fit for her prince — and such a handsome one too!' Her mother kissed her cheek and turned away, eager to make her way downstairs. 'You shall make your parents very proud, Elizabeth. I have waited a long time for this day to happen.' She almost sniffed away a tear.

'Mama, I wish to speak to you about the 'arrangements'. I am unclear about who it is I . . . ' Elizabeth's voice faded away as her mother stopped and faced her.

Her mother looked at her, the same expression she used on her as a child when she had asked an 'inappropriate question'. The excited air had dispersed momentarily, replaced by a sterner look of warning.

Elizabeth hesitated, then tilted her chin slightly upwards and continued to speak. 'I do not wish to cause anyone offence. However . . . '

'Elizabeth, if you are going to raise any girlish objections then please take time to think on them first. Learn to put such notions down to the nerves of a young girl and do not pay them lip-service to me. You are to be married to a fine man. Your father has worked and planned towards this moment for years. To undo his plans would be folly in the extreme and also very damaging.' The stern look on her mother's face softened and she smiled once more. 'What is more, Elizabeth dear, you will, in time, thank us dearly for the care we have taken in securing you a very suitable match, of that, I am quite sure.' Her mother smiled knowingly at Elizabeth, annoyingly even winking at her.

'Mama, why can I not go to London as you did?' Her question had been unexpected, she was sure for her mother looked quite shocked.

'That would be out of the question. You would be ridiculed, girl. No, it is not to be borne.' She was staring straight past Elizabeth to Dora.

'I know how to behave, Mama. Surely, I would not be an embarrassment to you?' Elizabeth saw her mother's bottom lip tremble slightly, and for one awful moment she thought her mother was going to say she was.

'Mr Seabright and I have always been proud to call you our daughter and we know that you would do nothing but make us pleased. However, London is London, and you are not educated in their way of thinking. People would talk, dear. We cannot dress you in the latest fashions, although we do our best. No, your father has given this matter a great deal of thought and he has decided to stay with the arrangements as made. This world can be exceedingly harsh; it is a world of which you rightfully know little, so do not press this issue further. You must be obedient and trust your father's better judgement.' Without waiting for a reply she continued swiftly on her way.

Elizabeth stormed into her room and flung the riding hat across the bed. She stamped her foot down firmly on the floor and looked in despair at Dora. 'I am not a child!' she announced. 'She still treats me as if I am.'

Dora said nothing but looked at Elizabeth's foot and raised a sardonic eyebrow.

Elizabeth blushed. 'You heard Mother. Go and fetch the water, Dora!' She watched her maid leave, a smile not even hidden on her face. Once she had gone, Elizabeth stamped her other foot firmly down, even harder than before, but in her boots it did nothing but make her foot ache. 'Childish,' she muttered and stared at her sulky reflection in the looking glass opposite. Perhaps they were correct after all, she mused. Was it time she accepted her fate?

Once clean and freshly attired, Elizabeth was bored with waiting for her summons to attend the gathering downstairs, so she decided to walk down the oak stairs and go to her father's library instead. Elizabeth had meant to call a servant and inform them where she was once there, but her eyes fell upon a book she had not seen before and at once started eagerly to read, expanding her growing knowledge of this fascinating world in which she lived, and yet, of which had seen so little. Within minutes she was settled in her father's favourite fireside chair and there curled her legs up underneath her muslin skirt, trying not to crease the new dress, and began to read. It was an escape Elizabeth loved to pursue, no matter how often her mother told her it was unbecoming of a young lady. Bookish women were supposed to be abhorrent to men, apparently. Elizabeth thought 'threatening' might be a better word — for wasn't knowledge a form of power in itself? Elizabeth believed it was and so she questioned her father on many issues, who had liked her to challenge his own vast understanding. Usually, he welcomed and approved of her hunger for knowledge and encouraged her outspoken ways — but not when it had prompted her to question his decision regarding the forthcoming betrothal. Her own future was planned and not to be either questioned or challenged. Only blind obedience was acceptable to him on this. She sighed and returned her thoughts to the book in hand.

To her dismay the library door was opened wide, a figure entered and then closed the doors securely behind him. The man walked casually over to the fire. He glanced around at the collection with interest. Then Mr Granger began to warm himself and, as she stared at him silently, it was as if he sensed her presence before he had seen her there. He took a step back as he suddenly turned to face her.

'I am sorry if I startled you, sir.' She spoke without hesitation and smiled at him not wanting to cause offence to her father's guest, yet, anxious to extricate herself from his company.

He returned her smile. 'Not in the least, Miss Elizabeth. I am delighted to have the pleasure of your company — so unexpectedly.' He glanced around the room appearing to be checking that they were, in fact, alone.

'To what do we owe the pleasure of your company, Mr Granger?' she said as confidently as she could and hoped her words also sounded innocent, whilst carefully straightening her legs out from underneath her skirt and sitting in a correct and dignified position. Elizabeth held her head high. She would never bow down to such a parasite as he, for that was how she viewed him — waiting for his chance to claim his, no doubt, large fee for his part in this ritual barter of money for a wife. He had none of her father's grace or humanity, she thought.

31

Instead, he seemed ill at ease in his manner and his costume. Elizabeth had often wondered what his mother, Lady Georgette, had been like but the lady was never mentioned in her presence. It was said, according to the gossip she had heard between Mrs Tully and Dora, that she married far beneath her and that is why he ended up working — albeit as a legal partner — for his living.

'Why?' he began to speak, then paused as he seemed to consider her closely for a second or two, lost in his own thoughts. He looked a little hesitant as he spoke, 'I am here to visit your father, Miss Elizabeth, upon the tender issue of the proposal.' His mouth formed a nervous half smile automatically as he spoke to her. 'I am hoping I find you feeling well . . . in both body and high spirit?' He looked at her thoughtfully.

'Yes, both are very well, sir.' She stood up rather abruptly. She noticed as she did so that he was a few years younger than she had always assumed him to be. For in the past she had not stood so close to him and his attire seemed to age him and accentuate his stature which, she could plainly see was that of an athletic frame. He held himself straight and proud. Elizabeth blushed slightly as she became aware that she had perhaps lingered too long as she pondered these facts.

'I am very pleased to hear it, Miss Elizabeth, for I had hoped to find you in the best of spirits.' He was smiling at her now, revealing a row of well formed white teeth.

'I did not expect you to find me at all. Surely, it is Father who you need to have your business concluded with?' She stared back at him, and could see he looked slightly bemused.

'I do . . . but are you not, or should I say, have you not been at all involved in the arrangements, Elizabeth?' He spoke quietly to her.

He was standing no more than six inches from her and his presence, so close, seemed to be having a strange affect upon Elizabeth's manner. 'Please do not concern yourself about my part in anything you and Father are arranging. In fact, I would rather not be a part of it at all.' She half smiled at the literal inference, pleased that she had thought of it. 'However, please refer to me as 'Miss' Elizabeth. It would show greater respect and I do not think, under the circumstances that we should appear in any way 'familiar'.'

He looked completely taken aback, but at the same time she could see he was gathering his thoughts quickly. He was taller than Elizabeth by a good head's height. Leaning slightly toward her, whilst speaking in a softly tone, he responded swiftly, 'Miss Elizabeth, I hold you in the greatest respect and shall always do so, despite your rather unfriendly manner.' She opened her mouth to protest but he merely shook his head and actually had the audacity to place a finger to her lips as if to silence a child. 'I shall not hold your outburst against you. But I will have you show me due respect too, miss. Then we shall become the best of friends as I do believe we need to be to enjoy our lives to their fullest.'

Her face was quite flushed as she stared, bewildered by the man's daring and almost smug countenance. She took two steps back from him. 'Don't you have more urgent business to attend to, sir, in York, Whitby or . . . the colonies?' Elizabeth asked sarcastically. 'You are normally too busy to waste your time talking with me or Mother on your visits to see Father,' she added, 'so why start now?'

He let out a long low breath before replying. Her words, she could see, had stung him like those she had uttered so carelessly to her aunt earlier. Elizabeth tried not to show her instant feelings of regret and so boldly held his stare.

'If you recall, Beth, it was you who was skulking in here. I did not come to you specifically.' He stood casually with one hand slipped under the tail of his coat.

'I do not 'skulk'. Good day, sir! I hope we will not have to meet again,' Elizabeth snapped at him, angry with her own poor behaviour and her inability in wit to outvoice this stranger. For in truth that was what he was. She had never before spoken to him, yet they were on the brink of becoming enemies.

'My dear child,' there was no mistaking this time his voice was deliberately patronising and calm which annoyed her intensely, 'I can assure you, I have much more important business here.' Mr Granger stared at her then raised his brow. 'You are curious, and I can see you know nothing of what is happening around you. Yet you are too proud to ask for all to be explained. You are charming, naïve and becoming, which must be very frustrating for you . . . Elizabeth. There are issues in relation to my inheritance that need addressing — nothing at all that has concerned you before — in any way. On that, dearest Elizabeth, you have my word. However, from this point onwards, everything changes and you cannot hide from it, for time is not on your side.'

'And I can assure you, Mr Granger, I have no wish to be involved in such discussions, as they will not be relevant to me.' Elizabeth held her composure, staring straight back into his eyes; they reminded her of the black local stone called Whitby jet. What thoughts lay behind them she tried not to guess at. Elizabeth took a step towards the doors, wanting to return to the safety of her maid, Dora.

'I hope all will be revealed to you soon, Elizabeth; for I am not at liberty to explain further.' Mr Granger walked around her, standing in front blocking her way to the doors behind him.

'I am not a servant girl who you can toy with at your will, sir!' Elizabeth was incensed by his attitude. She would not tolerate his intimidating behaviour now.

'Elizabeth, I do not 'toy' . . .' he paused to smile and then appeared to struggle to resume a more serious expression.

Elizabeth blushed deeper at her inappropriate words.

He continued in a more serious fashion ' . . . with servants or women in general. I wish that I could not talk in riddles to you, but perhaps if you would refrain from making such harsh judgements upon my person, soon your mother and father will explain the circumstances and then . . . '

'Move away from the door this minute or I shall scream!' Elizabeth put both hands on her hips and looked defiantly at him.

He sighed deeply again. 'Soon, miss, you will answer to me. I shall be in charge of you. Rest assured, I will expect better behaviour than you have displayed before me today!'

Elizabeth almost shook with frustration. She wanted to scream and shout out loud and do a myriad of other inappropriate behaviours. However, she would not lower her dignity further.

She would escape, though, and soon. Calming her voice she spoke plainly to him, 'Please, sir, let me pass as I have no wish to stay further.'

He nodded to her, stepped to the side and let her pass. As her hand found the door handle, he spoke softly to her. 'Elizabeth, think about what I have said.'

She slammed the door behind her as she left the room and continued at speed back to her bedchamber.

3

It was as she returned to her own room that she almost walked into her Aunt Jessica. Their eyes met. Elizabeth was still angry with her outburst against Mr Granger, but she knew she owed her aunt an apology.

'Aunt Jessica, I'm sorry I spoke thoughtlessly to you earlier. It is just that I am feeling agitated at the present time and I beg you to forgive my total insensitivity.' Her words were well chosen. Her manner, though, was still full of her previous angst.

'Well as long as you have got that off your chest then I suppose all should be well between us again. Your 'circumstances' are obviously more dire than that of your old ruined aunt.' Her words were icy, like her stare.

'I have apologised, Aunt Jessica, I really do mean it.' Elizabeth offered a hand to the woman who was staring at her. This time her manner was more genuine and her voice more sincere. 'You are a very attractive woman and far from old, Aunt.' Elizabeth saw her aunt was humoured and flattered by her last comment.

Jessica took the offered hand and led her into her own bedchamber. There she patted the settee next to her, inviting her headstrong niece to sit herself with her.

'What is it you do not feel happy about, girl?' Jessica asked, as she crossed her legs, rested an elbow upon her knee and leaned her head casually on her hand. 'Has your mother not explained to you what wifely duties will be expected of you?' She placed her head on one side as if she was encouraging her to share her inner most fears.

'No.' Elizabeth blushed and laughed at the thought of her mother trying to talk to her of anything to do with personal issues. 'No, she hasn't, Aunt, but it is not that which I . . . ' Elizabeth could see a glimmer of humour cross her aunt's eyes and decided it was best to change the subject quickly, for she had asked Dora all about babies and wifely duties. The maid, in her usual practical manner, had given her a graphical account of such things. In fact, more than Elizabeth had expected or desired to know. 'It is . . . well, everything. Tell me honestly what part, if any, does Mr Granger play in my future?' Elizabeth hesitated; she was feeling very uneasy. Her aunt could change mood as quickly as the weather. One minute the warmth of friendship on a summer's day, whilst the next, the cold chill of an icy wind across an exposed flat sandy beach.

'Why don't you ask your maid, Dora? I'm sure she knows more than we do about events. I have been here such a short time. After all, she has been your shadow throughout your life. If anyone knows the secrets of this family, the servants of longstanding will. Take my advice, Elizabeth, question her. Do not let her keep you in the dark any longer. If you do not want the man, Granger, as your suitor then you will have to react quickly. Believe me,' she shook her head, 'as you so rightly pointed out, I understand how an imperfect match can wreak havoc with a girl's fate.'

'No, it isn't Granger who is my suitor . . . it cannot be, he is just a lawyer and Father said he had found a man of rank, intelligence and experience. I presumed he was intending me to marry an older gentleman; possibly one of his friends.' Elizabeth swallowed, hating the thought, and looked up at her aunt's face. 'It can't be Granger, it mustn't be,' she declared as she glanced back at the door.

'Indeed it is, girl. Your father told me yesterday and would have spoken to you in more detail about events had you not stormed out of the room in a temper when he began to explain that your future, in a sense, was arriving today. He has not handled this well at all.' She laughed ironically adding, 'Then he is a man. Your poor mother follows his every word like a . . . ' she looked at Elizabeth's defensive glance and smiled sweetly, 'like a good wife should and has not spoken to you either. So now I shall, as much as I am able, or you shall turn away what could be the best proposal you have received, or indeed will ever.'

'I have not received any others,' Elizabeth replied.

'Yes, you have!' Jessica responded quickly. 'But your father has dismissed them for being too old, too rash or just plain unsuitable. He values you and that is why you should trust his judgement. Besides, you have little enough choice in the matter.' She patted Elizabeth's leg.

'Yes, I do,' Elizabeth replied quietly. 'I could run away!'

'Beth, are you out of your mind? You'd not survive on your own. You'd be ruined. Have you any idea what fate awaits a young woman on her own in the world. Your poor mother would never recover from the shock. Besides, if you did you could bring down your family and all that your father has striven to achieve. No, the idea is too bad. You must put it out of your head and make the best of your situation. If the man is a total dote then I shall try and intervene in the matter, but at least give him a chance.' She stood up. 'Now, off with you, I have been understanding enough for one day. Do not test my good nature further for it has been in short enough supply in recent months.'

She stood up, but then Jessica slipped her hand in hers. 'Listen, Beth, it may be hard for a woman in this world with a man, but it is nigh impossible to exist without one unless you have a family to love and care for you. I could have so very easily ended up on the streets myself.' Her eyes were moist as her hand fell away to her lap. 'Life on the streets for any woman is cruel, for a noble woman it would beyond tolerance — although some have had to.'

'Father would never have allowed that,' Elizabeth answered as she bent and for the first time kissed her aunt lightly on the cheek. 'You are too much a lady for that to be even contemplated.'

'That is precisely my point, Beth. He wouldn't, and neither will he see you harmed, so trust in him.'

Beth gave her a little nod and opened the door without saying a further word, where she was left once more to her own thoughts.

Elizabeth entered her own bedchamber to see a very red-faced mother waiting for her on the window seat. 'Whatever is wrong, Mama?' Elizabeth rushed over to her expecting some fearful bad news.

'Why, nothing dear. It is just that I wish to have a talk with you. I have not discussed certain things openly with you before and I feel it is time that I did. I am your mother and as such it is my duty to prepare you.' She patted the cushioned seat next to her. Elizabeth dutifully sat down, she could not help but contrast the differences between her practical aunt and her mother's somewhat ethereal manner.

Pollyana cleared her throat then took in a deep breath. 'When you take a husband, Beth,' she said softly, then immediately glanced out of the window as if looking for inspiration, her cheeks flushed bright crimson, 'or when a man takes a wife — it does not have to be . . . awkward or difficult. It can be pleasant or, on occasion, enjoyable.' She stood up and held her daughter's hands in hers. 'You do not need to fear what is a natural act between a man and a woman because a good man will show you how things are . . . done. What is more it is your duty, so all shall be fine.' She let out what appeared to be a sigh of relief and smiled nervously. 'Now, has that put your fears to rest?' Her mother's smile grew in warmth as Elizabeth silently nodded.

'Good.' She let loose her daughter's hands apparently satisfied that her awkward moment of motherly duty had been despatched successfully.

'Mother, may I ask you a question?'

The smile dropped and the nervous look reappeared on the older woman's face. 'If you must, I suppose.'

'Why did you not tell me before, that it was Mr Granger himself that you have made arrangements with and that he is not acting on behalf of another? Why would father choose him?' Elizabeth tried to remove all temper from her voice in order to gain the knowledge she desired.

Her mother's apprehension returned instantly.

'Well, Elizabeth, that is not one but two questions.' She pursed her lips and breathed deeply again, her colour fuller than ever Elizabeth had seen it before. 'He is a fine young man and we thought you would accept our choice without question. It never occurred to either of us that you would create such a fuss. You've always been a dutiful daughter, Beth. Don't change now. Meet Mr Granger properly. I shall arrange for him to walk with you tomorrow in the gardens and you may then discuss your future with him openly whilst I watch from the morning room. I am sure you two will be perfect for each other. He is a family friend of long standing, darling.' She kissed her daughter on her cheek. 'Now, you think on what I have told you and stop this worrying. You should be happy, for your own life is about to start as a woman and soon you shall have the joy of daughters of your own. Then we shall talk as one woman to another. Beth, I hope you will be as happy as I am with your father.'

Elizabeth watched her mother leave. Guilt flooded through her. What had she done other than acted like a fool in front of the man she was set to spend the rest of her life with. Tomorrow she would walk in the gardens, and under Mama's scrutiny, they would have to be civil to each other and she would be expected to perform as a model of charm itself.

She cringed and held her head in her hands. 'Damn that man!' she muttered, but inside her anger was purely reserved for her own inability to accept with grace the future she must.

4

'Dora!'

Her maid entered the room, shutting the door behind her and staring at her mistress. 'Are they ready for you to join them now, miss?' she asked, and walked straight over to her mistress who was seated by her looking glass. Automatically she started to tidy a couple of wispy loose ends that had escaped her combs.

Elizabeth waved her away with a flick of her hand. 'I want you to answer a few questions. There are things going on in my home that I do not understand and before I face my father, and that man, I will know what they are!' She stood up straightening her back as she had seen Jessica do when she was riled, and looked down at Dora, who for once seemed ill at ease. Her hand shook as it positioned her comb back onto the dressing table.

'Miss Elizabeth, I think you are imagining things. Your father will answer all your questions, I'm sure.' She turned her head away as she spoke leaving Elizabeth with that same growing sense of unease within her that her aunt's words had.

'Dora, tell me please.' She placed her hand on Dora's shoulder and made her face her. 'What is the connection between Mr Granger and Father?'

'Miss, it's not my place to say . . . anything. I've been with you since you were a babe in arms. Please do not make me say what is none of my concern. I . . . have to go. You'll be called soon, I'm sure.' Dora tried to pull away.

'No! Tell me who this man is to Father and why should I have not had any say in the match. Dora you must know if there is a family secret. What far reaching shadows are hanging over me and my family?' Elizabeth held her firmly.

'Miss, I will not say a thing because it

is not my place to.' Dora's eyes were moist.

'Then you leave me no choice. I shall leave because, if I don't, I shall not have another chance to.'

Dora's expression changed from fear to anger at her words. 'You'd be selfish and foolish to try! I have work to do. Please, excuse me, miss.'

Elizabeth took a step toward her bedchamber doorway where Dora was still holding the door handle.

'You should not speak to me like that! I'm your mistress!' Elizabeth felt that her position in life was slipping away.

Dora did not look at her. 'Aye, I suppose you are and I'm a fool to think I was anythin' more than your maid,' Dora muttered and walked out.

'Dora Root, come back here this minute!' Elizabeth shouted along the hall but her maid, her friend, had descended down the servants' stairs to where Elizabeth herself had told her she belonged.

Elizabeth was left alone and, as she returned to her bedchamber and studied her reflection in the looking glass, a feeling of disgust surged through her as she remembered her behaviour to Mr Granger a moment ago and, more importantly, to Dora. What was happening to her? Where was the happy carefree spirit she had always known? She felt trapped. She would never obey him. She would fulfil her duty to her parents and no more. The time had come for her to leave her childlike world behind; she could no longer be protected from the truth, whatever it was. It had found her.

Mr Granger had said that she would answer to him. That idea was too preposterous to be borne, he was a stranger. She had always believed whatever Dora had told her. The woman knew something about her past that she did not. For the first time in Elizabeth's life she felt empty and alone. She was frightened and distressed by Mr Granger's advice. Staring at herself in the glass, she saw someone she had never looked upon clearly before.

Elizabeth was not given to petulance or sulking, yet she had displayed both in the space of a day and upset some of the closest people to her. Somehow, she would find her way in to see her father one more time, and then if he would not speak reasonably to her, reluctantly she would leave. Elizabeth decided she would head for York first, and one thing was certain, Dora Root was going to accompany her; for without her there was no reason to employ her as a personal maid.

★　★　★

Granger awoke early the next morning annoyed that the evening had not passed off better. His intended had displayed a side of her character he had not witnessed previously, although from a distance he had admired her for years, and what is more, she sat almost in silence throughout dinner. Her embarrassed parents had made very interesting conversation, hinting that she was overwhelmed and tired by events after being caught out in the rain and needed a good night's rest.

As he rode across the open fields, loving the feeling of being in the country once more, yet so near to the tempestuous sea, he pondered what Miss Elizabeth really needed to teach her some good manners. He grinned at the prospect for he had judged her correctly. She was a woman of character and that was why he would go through with his father's wishes.

He approached a village and thought he saw a gathering forming in the main square. Deciding he and his horse both needed a refreshing drink after the gallop, he rode over to a stone trough outside a small inn, and dismounted. People looked on, nervous and edgy. It was only as he entered the square leading his horse to the water that he saw the three mounted soldiers on horseback facing them. He listened to the unfolding conversation and stroked his horse's neck as it drank.

One soldier looked down at a man wearing the black robes of a preacher; the man spoke loudly to him. 'In God's Holy name stop this atrocity before someone is really hurt!' The man was brave and stood boldly in front of a small gathering of men, women and children who had grouped behind him.

'Listen, Reverend. I respect you. You think you are doing God's work here but you're not. You're encouraging the rabble to revolt. Now step aside and I'll be about my business then we can all get on with our own lives, instead of meddling in other folk's. What do you say, man?'

The preacher man held up his Bible to the red jacketed figure sitting upon the horse in front of him. It riled Granger that such an uncouth lout could wear the uniform that represented his country. 'Is it your business to arrest men for listening to the Word of our Lord?'

Granger reflected that the man had a very good point and an educated voice in which to state it.

'Don't give me that unless you want to come to the lock-up with them, named and shamed as a leader. They're machine breakers, we know it and, what's more, you know it too. So let's stop playing games and you find some other sheep to worry.' He laughed at his own quip and walked his horse directly at the man in black.

The priest stood tall; his broad shoulders did not sag or cower. He held his back straight. His blonde shoulder-length hair rested on the black uniform he wore but, like Granger himself, it was not the only part of him that was in stark contrast to his clothes. He saw the man's defiance as he stared back at the soldier and his two colleagues as they drew their swords and walked forwards.

'Go inside,' the priest ordered the women and children, and gladly they obeyed, whilst he and three unarmed mill workers stood to face the mounted men. The horse's head was brought level with the priest's whilst the man's sword was pointed at his chest.

'Gentlemen, isn't this state of affairs getting out of hand?' Granger spoke up having let go of his horse's reins. He was dressed in the riding outfit of a gentleman and not for once in his own black dour uniform.

The soldier looked to him and appeared quite unimpressed at what he saw. 'Sir, with due respect, be about your business.'

Granger had walked to within a few yards of the soldier, carrying his crop in his hand. For a brief moment he considered using it to strike the obnoxious sergeant's horse, but he liked horses, so he decided he would rather use it on the man himself given half a chance or reason.

The soldier saw no threat from him so continued to harangue the priest. 'You have either faith in abundance or more than your share of stupidity, man. Do you think that uniform gives you protection from the law?' the soldier asked him.

'No, I do not, but tell me, sir . . . ' the priest began to answer.

'Could you answer the same question, sir? Do you presume yours does?' Granger responded, interrupting the man and preventing him letting out his anger on the priest.

This time the man's attention focussed upon him. 'You insolent wretch! Who in hell's name do you think you are? Or perhaps you are one of them — their leader?' he suggested and the eyes of his men turned toward him. Granger could see that the men behind the priest were edgy, ready to break into a run. The whole situation needed to be diffused.

'No sir, I am a man of the law and I obviously understand it a damn sight more than you. If these men are guilty of some offence they will be tried fairly. Let me talk to them and I will advise them as to their rights.' Granger saw a look of distaste cross the sergeant's face.

'Rights man — they have no rights

— they broke the law. Get them!' The man's order was instantly obeyed.

The three men panicked and ran. 'No!' Granger shouted and the priest joined in his unheeded plea. Both understood that the men's action had condemned them, as no man could outrun a horse. The soldier swung his sword at Granger, trying to injure him, but he responded like the priest, and moved swiftly. Granger took only a light cut to the wrist. The pain was sharp but so were his wits. He grabbed the man's sleeve and unsaddled him. The sergeant hit the ground with a heavy thud, the wind knocked out of his body.

Granger mounted the sergeant's horse and pointed to his own horse telling the preacher to ride it. The man obeyed and jumped astride the horse, kicking it on into a gallop, riding after the other two soldiers. He followed after the men. They had caught up with their prey and had used their musket butts to beat the men down. One lay groaning and had blood seeping from his head.

'What justice is this?' Granger shouted as he approached them.

'Ours,' answered one, and raised his sword. 'You can join them seeing as you're so interested in their souls.' He rode towards Granger who sat upon his mount and waited for his moment to strike. As the man neared, he sleekly dismounted, smacking the horse's rump so it trotted off in the direction of the mill workers.

'Kneel, whoever you are!' the man laughed, and his confidence grew. His friend looked on. 'You should learn to keep your nose out of official business.'

Granger bent a knee slightly as if he was going to obey. His fist tightened into a firm ball. 'Please, God, if it is your will, let it be done . . . ' He punched out sideways as he knelt, the horse reared and the man toppled from it. His newly made friend dismounted and ran over to help him. He grabbed the fallen man's sword in his hand and met his attacker's blow with equal force. It was only a matter of minutes before he had disarmed him. Granger and the priest held them at sword point long enough for the mill workers to escape to the cover of the woods where at least they would have a fighting chance. Their families would not see them again — well, not for long enough, but better that than see them dance at the end of a rope, condemned as Luddites.

Granger mounted his horse; the priest climbed on behind him before they threw the sergeant's sword to the ground.

'A priest and a horse thief!' one of the men shouted in fury and frustration at the situation he found himself in.

'Good day, 'gentlemen'.'

Granger galloped off down the road and, after he had travelled for half an hour he returned the priest to his lodgings at the Badger's Beck Inn. He had left the horse in the yard and collected the man's bag from his room. God appeared to be with this man today as the coach was due to leave for

Newcastle within the half hour. The soldiers would not complete their journey for at least two, and by then they would both be gone.

'Would you be all right now, Reverend?' Granger asked.

'Yes, and thank you, sir. I was travelling north when I came across those hapless chaps.'

'Were they guilty?' Granger asked.

'Would you have helped if they were?' the priest asked.

'I am a man of the law; it is my role in life to follow the rules.' Granger saw a flash of a smile upon the priest's face.

'I like to think it is my role to see justice done, also. So let us just say we did that.' He shook Granger's hand.

'Thank you.' He offered the man some money to pay for his safe journey to Newcastle and it was taken gratefully.

Granger fastened his riding coat and, leaving his new friend sitting on a wall, he waved and rode off.

5

Elizabeth approached the edge of the woods that separated the marsh land that bordered the flat sands and the moor road with the villages in the dales beyond. She had had a fitful sleep and decided she needed to ride whilst still at liberty to choose to without seeking the permission of the man, Granger. She could not imagine the 'desk-clerk' enjoying such pursuits. Elizabeth smiled as she conjured up in her mind an image of him bent over a desk, quill in hand, surrounded by dusty ledgers. Her smile faded when she sketched an outline of herself standing behind him, for wouldn't that be her role in life should she fill it?

Elizabeth followed the path which led up through the woods to the moors and the village of Hazelholme. It was only a small hamlet but she liked the people there and often stopped to let her horse take a drink from the village's stone trough. As she approached a clearing half way along the track that led her up through the woods, she saw a bedraggled figure running toward her. The man clearly in a panic and sweating profusely had a trickle of blood running down his brow. He stumbled erratically off the path and fell headlong into a cluster of tall ferns. Elizabeth walked her horse as near to him as she could without leading it off the path. She was about to dismount and see if she could help him when another figure appeared in the distance. This time it was the outline of a red jacket that stood out from the woodland cover. The man in the undergrowth groaned loudly. 'They'll hang me!' his voice said pathetically. 'Help me for mercy's sake!'

'Stay still, man, and remain deathly quiet. I'll see if I can send him on his way.' Elizabeth rode toward the soldier to offer a distraction from the hapless figure who had collapsed on the cold earth. She had no notion as to whether her actions were the correct ones but prayed she was doing the right thing. What on earth had happened to him? What had the man done?

'Morning, sir,' she addressed the soldier as he ran and stumbled towards her.

'Morning, ma'am,' he answered, and puffed as he fought to breathe evenly. Another soldier appeared behind him.

'Pardon, but this is not a safe place for a young lady to be out riding on her own,' the older soldier advised her.

'Why ever not? It is a beautiful day, sir, and I frequently ride on these paths.' She smiled sweetly and looked around her affectionately at the woodland.

'There are machine-breakers afoot, ma'am,' he continued, 'men who would take advantage of a pretty young miss, such as yourself.' He winked at his friend and Elizabeth began to feel most unsure of her own safety.

'Well, no one has passed by me, or I should have seen or heard them. There are no machines around these parts to break, are there?' she asked innocently, knowing full well that many of the cottagers were irate about their home industry being taken away from them by big manufactories and their greedy mill owners further west and south of them. Dora had said more than once that is was unfair and short-sighted of the men who built them.

'They run like rats scattering to the rivers and woodlands to escape justice.' He turned to the other soldier. 'Damn it, man. They've got clean away. I'd like to get my hands on that bloody priest and the interferin' gentleman who was in league with him! We best be on our way back to barracks. It'll take us the best part of a day; we'll find an inn . . . ' his manner changed from anger to wit as he laughed and side-glanced at Elizabeth, 'and a good woman to keep us warm en route.' The sergeant winked at the other man. 'Or even better, a bad one,' he added, then he too glanced at a very uneasy Elizabeth.

'Sir, you are embarrassing the lady,'

his friend said and openly laughed at her.

The sergeant walked over to her. 'Whereabouts are you from, miss? You see, we are just passing through this area and not really known around these parts. We would appreciate it if you would climb down off that horse and show us around.' He placed his hand on her leg. She grabbed her crop but he held her hand firmly pre-empting her intention to strike him.

'I would appreciate it if you would leave my fiancée alone and be on your way before I plant you next to one of these trees.' The voice bellowed down through the trees and both men turned with fear on their faces, as they had been caught with both their pistols and muskets unloaded.

Elizabeth also looked shaken and stared at the man who had appeared on the higher ground. Mr Granger was standing on the upper path pointing a rifle at the sergeant's body.

Elizabeth backed her horse a little

way down the path slowly so as to distance her from the soldiers.

'You again!' the sergeant shouted. 'I'll have you whipped for your insolence!' His voice was so irate that it almost cracked as he replied.

'Not whilst you are in my sights you won't. Leave your guns on the ground and run for the moors. Keep going until you return to the place you were unleashed onto this unsuspecting world from and do not come back. I have friends in high places and you two would be as easy to remove to the front line in Spain as an ant from my boot. Now run!' He let one bullet whistle past the sergeant's ear. Elizabeth's horse fidgeted uneasily but she controlled it well as the two frightened men left their precious weapons and ran as if the devil himself were after them.

Elizabeth watched Granger's hawk-like vigil as he kept to his place until seemingly sure the men had kept going beyond the distant ridge. Then he walked his own horse through the woodland, picking his path carefully until he could join Elizabeth on the lower trod.

She was quite speechless. As she watched this man approach, so different in attire and manner to the desk-clerk she had upset in the library, she could have believed him to be a complete stranger to her. This man was daring, worldly — dangerous even.

Elizabeth was about to smile up at him as he neared her but then she remembered the poor soul in the ferns and was dumb-struck. Mr Granger was a man of the law and this man had broken it. What should she do?

★ ★ ★

Jessica looked at the mahogany door that stood between her and her brother's office. She held her head erect and tried the handle. The door was locked. She felt a presence at her side. Glancing sideways she saw that standing facing her was her sister-in-law.

Pollyana's delicate white muslin gown accentuated the flush pink of her cheeks. 'Can I help you, dear sister?' she asked Jessica sweetly.

'I wish to see my brother,' Jessica said rather obviously, and watched Pollyana nervously pick at the fine embroidery on her sleeve. The high-waisted dress was one of her finest and it suited her slender figure. Jessica hoped that Pollyana would be touched by her predicament, understanding that she may need to discuss issues privately with her brother and so let them speak on their own for a few precious moments.

'I'm sorry, Jessica, dear, but he is dressing for his meeting with Timothy, and is not to be disturbed. I have been instructed that he wants to have his mind clear when he welcomes the young man into the family . . . officially.' Pollyana blushed slightly.

Jessica lowered her head slightly, but her eyes never flinched as they stared defiantly at Polyanna's. 'Why phrase it so, Polly? What is this man? A clerk, a partner of a prestigious law firm or does he have some stronger connection with this family? I have a right to know.'

Pollyana's face changed from a pleasant relaxed expression to one of agitation. 'Do you? This matter is of no concern to you. He is the man chosen to be Elizabeth's husband and as such, my husband's decision is beyond question!' she almost snapped back her words which surprised Jessica and only led her to be more concerned for her niece's future. What was her brother doing?

Jessica looked at her sister-in-law. 'Polly, I do not question the choice, just asking for an explanation as to what is happening around me.'

'Well, perhaps it is not your place to ask, Jessica!' Pollyanna looked as though her outburst had shocked herself. 'Luncheon will be served promptly, please do not be late.' She trembled slightly and turned away as if she had dismissed a servant.

Jessica stared at Pollyana's back until the woman was out of sight. Her fists formed into balls at her side and she nodded slowly. Her brother would speak to her, of that she was sure, and soon.

6

'I think it would be advisable for us to make ourselves scarce, Elizabeth,' Granger spoke confidently as he brought his horse alongside hers.

She looked up at him, hardly able to believe the transformation from the black clad 'desk-clerk' to this person who now presented himself to her. She glanced at the rifle, which he had placed alongside his saddle.

A man groaned and he instantly clasped the weapon in his hand once more.

'No, don't shoot him. He is already injured. They,' Elizabeth pointed along the path in the direction the men had run, 'those men were chasing him,' Elizabeth explained, knowing this was not a reason for her to hide a fugitive from the law, but having no option than to say something in explanation.

Granger handed her his horse's reins and dismounted. He picked up the soldiers' unloaded weapons and hid them under a log as he walked past them on the path. 'I shall return for them later.' Without hesitation he made his way to the fallen man. Granger raised him up; the man looked delirious. Lifting him bodily over his shoulder, he brought him to the horse. Without speaking to either the man or Elizabeth he helped him into the saddle and climbed up behind him.

'We must go from here, and quickly.' He kicked the horse onwards.

Elizabeth glanced back for any sign of the soldiers returning. She was relieved when there was no glimmer of red jackets reappearing through the trees, but still she was anxious and followed Granger as he broke into a gallop, supporting the injured man, as he traversed the open flat sands. Instead of heading back toward the estate he was riding in the opposite direction straight for the Coble Inn which had been built on the edge of the beach under the shadow of the headland of Stangcliffe.

They did not stop nor slow down until they approached the soft sand outside the inn. The cluster of fishermen's cottages, boats and nets nestled around and behind it. Once outside, Granger slipped out of his saddle and let the man slide into his arms as he had no strength to hold himself upright.

Again Elizabeth held the reins and silently looked on as Granger carried his burden inside the inn. It was some moments before he reappeared.

He seemed ill at ease as he brushed off some mud from his jacket and remounted his horse.

'We shall leave now because this is no place for you to be seen.' They cantered along the beach following the line of the grass-covered dunes. The noise of waves breaking in the distance and gulls kwaarking overhead did not distract Elizabeth from her thoughts. She rode ahead of him, stopping her horse across his path, staring at the enigma of a man who was silently escorting her back to her home.

He reined in and looked at her.

'I think, sir, you owe me some explanation of what has happened here.' She had not meant to sound confrontational but her words had left her lips with a sharper tone than she had intended.

'Do I?' he asked, smiling at her. His expression was so animated and full of life it was as though he was a completely different character to the one he presented at the hall.

'You knew that man!' She realised that was the thing that had annoyed her about him . . . this time. He had not asked Elizabeth who the man was, or how he had got there. Granger had taken one look at him and lifted him to a place of safety. It was as if no answers were needed, so therefore he had knowledge of the man's circumstance. How?

'Not personally, but I was aware of

his plight.' His answer sounded almost smug.

Elizabeth stared beyond Granger back to the inn. Even at this distance she could make out the figures of fishermen as, hurriedly, they launched a coble onto the waves.

Granger turned his head and then looked back at her. 'He will be safe now. They'll take him to one of the bay towns and there he can recover from his ordeal.'

'He was an outlaw so why would a man of the law help him?' Elizabeth asked, and caught a look of humour cross his eyes.

'Why would a lady hide him from the King's soldiers?' he responded, and walked his horse alongside hers so he was looking her straight in the eye.

'I wasn't . . . not exactly,' she hesitated.

'Yes, Elizabeth, you were and I applaud you for it, because those men were bullies in uniform. They did not uphold the law as it is supposed to be carried out. The man has lost his liberty to be with his family. He will live watching over his shoulder in fear that he is caught. However, he has now got a chance to survive.'

She had not expected him to compliment her at all.

'You acted nobly,' she replied quietly.

He could not help himself laugh at her. 'Did it hurt you so much to say something positive about me, Beth? Is your dislike of me so intense?' His humour dissipated.

'You are very familiar, sir,' she replied quickly.

'Why do you dislike me so, when you know nothing about me?' His smile had disappeared and she felt the sincerity in his words.

'I do not dislike you . . . '

'Don't you?' he asked without hesitation.

'I don't know you. I know nothing about you. You have appeared at regular intervals over the past few years dressed in funereal style and somehow your presence upsets my parents.'

'Does it indeed?' he asked, again a note of surprise within his voice.

She ignored him. 'Then I discover you are to be my husband and I have not so much as been introduced to you. What is more, I am supposed to accept this without question.' Elizabeth could feel her cheeks flush red, despite the cold sea air that stung them.

'Yes, as a dutiful daughter, it is your duty to.' He looked at her sternly, the countenance of the desk-clerk returning.

Elizabeth took in a sharp breath and controlled her response. 'As an educated woman, with a mind of my own I shall tell you now, sir. I will not!'

He shook his head. 'You are so easy to rile, woman. I shall talk to your father when I return and ask if we may be given some time on our own to sort issues out. Then you will be more conducive to the idea, I am certain.' He stared at her.

'Are you?' she answered him dryly.

'Yes,' he smiled.

'Well, I shall speak to Father because I am not! Good day, sir.'

She cantered off and soon heard the breath of his horse as he approached alongside her. They galloped, side by side, the wind in their faces. Apparently a race had begun and Granger's face was almost laughing as his animal was superior to hers and annoyingly took the lead, riding ahead of her as he led the way back to her home.

7

Jessica fumed silently for an hour. This hall had been her home once. She fully understood that her brother had the rights of inheritance but being talked to in such a manner by Pollyanna hurt her pride deeply. She had long suspected that Silas's wife — 'lap dog' — had resented her strength of will and forthright manner. She was even coming to suspect that Pollyanna was quietly delighted that her sister-in-law's marriage had fallen into ruin. Herbert had taken to excessive drinking with his friends at his London club, but then most men did. However, in those moments he was good humoured enough. It was not this that had destroyed his character, Jessica admitted to herself at least; it had been opium which had been his ultimate downfall. Yet, before his 'friends' had introduced him to these ruinous dens in the bowels of London, they had been a carefree, child free and happily married couple. He had always been a little reckless and she had loved him for it because of the freedom that she had experienced with him, until one day he returned from one of his delirium filled visits, out of his senses and had struck her hard. With that one blow her love and patience were shattered and she had returned to her erstwhile home, until he sorted himself out. She was wracked with guilt, but after a year of reasoning and pleading with him he still would not listen to her. It had gone too far. Her own safety was at stake.

Now, returning to the home she had loved as a child, Jessica felt as though she had taken the place of a house-keeper; to be consulted over domestic arrangements but to be subservient to Pollyana, and ever grateful to her brother, Silas. At least the girl, Elizabeth, had spirit and she liked that because it reminded her of her own opinionated ways, but her situation was becoming as stifling and intolerable as Elizabeth's own dilemma was to her.

Jessica decided she would not be fobbed off by her brother any longer. She walked along to his bedchamber. Pollyana had the room next door, Jessica half smiled to herself; she had always shared her husband's bed, happily, until . . . Her smile faded.

She reached behind the chair that was placed next to it. Her father had always kept a spare key there in case he forgot his own. She was sure that her brother had kept the same habit. He had emulated her father in every other way. Silas would be appalled if he knew that Jessica had thought her father weak. If he was avoiding her she would confront him in his own quarters.

Jessica was about to place the key in the lock when she heard Pollyana talking to a servant on the stairs. She slipped into the room opposite leaving the door slightly ajar and watched.

'Go to the kitchens now, you can

clean later. I wish to speak with Mr Seabright.' Jessica saw the servant walk away and Pollyanna nervously enter Silas's room. She knocked twice and heard her brother turn the key in the lock, then shout, 'enter.' Once the woman was inside and the door was firmly closed behind her Jessica crept across the landing and listened silently by the door.

'Pollyana! What on earth are you doing in here? I told you to wait for me in the morning room. Timothy has gone out riding and I want to speak with him first; you should be talking to that daughter of yours!' His voice was harsh. 'She will not humiliate me in front of Timothy.'

'Silas, dear, I am glad to see you are looking somewhat better than your mood of last evening. I came up, dear, to talk with you ... not about Elizabeth, she is just understandably nervous. I'm sure she will see sense soon.'

'It had better be very soon because I

will not have Timothy treated like this. He is entitled to this estate as well you know. If he does not marry Elizabeth and stand in line to claim the estate when we are . . . well . . . when the time is right, he could insist on us being turned out now. What if he were to meet another more conducive female? Then where would we be? No better than that dim-witted sister of mine!'

'Shh!' Pollyanna said quickly, 'she mustn't hear you talk of such things.'

'Do you think she is listening at the door, woman?' Silas asked sarcastically and Jessica continued to listen amazed at the words she was hearing.

'No, of course not, dear, but she does want to know things. She has asked me questions and I find her presence here very disturbing, my dear. She walks around as if she owns the hall and I am belittled by it. Can we not find somewhere else for her to stay?' Pollyanna's voice was as clear as could be.

Jessica was in no doubt how the

calculating mind of this woman was working.

'What does she want to know, Polly?' he asked.

'I think it may be she who is poisoning Elizabeth's mind against marriage. After all, dear, her own marriage went so very wrong and you know how jealousy can sometimes distort a woman's mind.' She coughed delicately.

Jessica's fists were clenched tight. She wanted to burst in and vent her rage but if she did they were in their right to cast her out. No, she would be more devious than that. Jessica decided she had heard enough. It was time she used her mind to sort out her own problems. But why should this man, Granger, hold such power over her brother?

There were questions to be answered, but firstly she would have to guard against the accusations being made against her by her own jealous sister-in-law.

★ ★ ★

Elizabeth was extremely peeved that the man had ridden ahead of her. She felt foolish, yet again, and frustrated that she could not even have the opportunity to speak with her own father before him. She saw the gates of the estate in the distance and slowed her horse from a gallop to a walk. For she would not be seen entering in an undignified manner. She would take her time. The race was lost; he had the finer animal, so she would at least arrive unflustered. She entered the grounds as calmly as she could.

'Should we be seen riding in side by side, as if in a truce, Elizabeth?' The deep voice resounded from where he, Granger, had sheltered his horse under an old oak tree just inside the grounds.

Elizabeth was surprised — pleasantly so, but did not want to show it. 'Do you enjoy toying with people, sir?' she asked.

'That is the second time you have accused me of it in so many days. My name is Timothy, please use it.' He joined her and held out a hand.

She glanced warily at it. 'I do not know what to make of you . . . Timothy. For years you have appeared to be one thing and yet I see before me a totally different person. What am I to think of you?'

He relaxed his hand and placed it back upon the reins of the horse. 'Think of me what you will as you allow yourself time to know me, but be careful of prejudging a person. It is a dangerous thing to do and is so often unfair.'

He gestured that they should walk on, so for once Elizabeth did as she was bid, pleased that he had the good manners to at least wait for her. However, she would soon speak with her father.

8

Jessica was seething. She listened to them talking until her brother said to his wife, 'I shall come to you tonight, be ready.'

'Yes dear,' came the dutiful reply.

Jessica returned to her own room to collect her shawl. She thought of her own husband, who had always been with her, every night of their married life unless he was at the club. How she had ached for his presence. She was wracked with loneliness and guilt. Marriage was for better or worse, yet she had run away. She was broken in spirit because the passion, the love they had shared, had been replaced by his demons.

It was hard for her to cry. She had always been strong. Their father had taught her to be. Crying brought more rebukes, more smacks from the cane.

Even now she flinched at the memory of his discipline. Yet, in her husband's arms she had been loved, and yet it ended with the pain of a beating. How could she ever forgive him? No, that was wrong. She could forgive him almost anything but could not forget that.

She had to breathe the fresh air. Jessica stormed out of Marshend with her shawl wrapped tightly around her shoulders.

It was time for her to think of a way out of the mess her husband had left her in. The last time she had seen him he had been in yet another drug-filled stupor, not even remembering the violent acts of the night before. How could she stay with a man who had succumbed to that kind of behaviour? Silas had understood her position and her actions. He had had his fill of beatings and had sworn that no child of his would suffer the same fate. Of that he had been true to his word.

One month after leaving, her love

had neither sent her word to rebuke her nor visited the hall to beg her to return. Was she destined to be a charity case for the rest of her life?

She saw two riders approaching down the drive and realised one of them was Elizabeth. The girl was fine, spirited and strong. Jessica hoped no man broke that spirit.

Pollyanna had accused her of swaying Elizabeth's mind. Perhaps, Jessica toyed with the idea, maybe she should. Why not? If she were a bitter resentful woman she would, just to have her revenge upon Pollyanna. However, Silas deserved better. She would not let him down in such a manner. But more worrying was the comment that they could lose the manor. How? What claim did the man, Granger, have over it?

Jessica did not want to be seen so she stepped into the shadows and made her way behind the building. She saw the stables and wondered if she should make herself scarce until the riders had dismounted. Her sight had not been strong enough to make out with whom Beth was riding. A smile crossed her face. Perhaps the girl had a reason for not wanting to marry — perhaps she had her heart already set on a man of her own choice. Jessica waited for the riders to come closer as she stood just inside the stable block. This Timothy person had some claim to the manor house, Jessica was attracted to dark horses and he promised to be a very handsome one.

* ★ *

'I don't understand why you, a man of the world, would want to marry me, a woman you do not know!' Elizabeth had stopped her horse and was watching him closely. She aimed to shock him to see what reaction she could stir in this man who had always acted with propriety.

'I have not proposed to you so how do you know for certain that I do, Elizabeth?' He looked at her with humour.

'You must be serious! For years you have been, so why change now?' she asked and his smile disappeared, to be replaced by a very serious expression. 'The answer is simple. Everything has changed now. I am twenty-five. I have made my name and fulfilled all that was assigned to me to achieve. Now I no longer have to bow and scrape. I have the law on my side and I fully intend to use it should anyone renege on the agreement. There is much that should have been explained to you, Elizabeth. The truth is that neither of us have any say in this marriage. It is one that was arranged by our fathers and grand-fathers as soon as you were accepted by Silas.'

Elizabeth raised an eyebrow as he referred to her father in such a familiar way.

'It would be extremely unfortunate for your family if it fell through and ruin-ous for me also. So let us be determined to make the best of the situation and at least decide to tolerate each other.'

His words surprised her and she stared at him as there was no humour in his expression at all. 'That explains nothing!' Elizabeth snapped, her voice full of frustration. 'One minute you act like a desk-clerk, the next like a soldier threatening men with a rifle. You are an enigma, sir. I wish to marry a man I can trust and who I have feelings for. Not one who is everything to everybody and who talks in riddles.'

'I am what I have had to be.' He rode his horse next to hers looking at her, his face so close to hers as he spoke with what appeared to be open sincerity. 'You have been very fortunate, Elizabeth. You have grown up here in this estate which by right should have been mine.'

Elizabeth stared at him open mouthed, wanting to speak and refute this claim but feeling the man was passionate about what he had said. There was a cold reality within his words which stung her.

'You believe me. That is good

because you will soon learn that I am a man who speaks his mind. I will not live a lie, not any more. I am here to claim my birthright, and you, Elizabeth, are part of it. I shall honour the marriage as it was agreed and I shall also claim my bride.' He gently closed her mouth with the tip of his finger under her chin. 'I deeply desire us to be friends, for there has been enough animosity between our families over the years. I have watched and admired you from a distance through time, knowing one day you would be my bride. So accept our destiny and thank God that you were taken in by such a charitable man.' He smiled at her.

Elizabeth felt the anger return within her. 'What? Why would you say such a thing?' She stared at him through puzzled and irate eyes. 'Whatever do you mean, taken in?'

'You did not know?' It was his turn to look abashed. 'Elizabeth . . . I am sorry. I would have not said such a thing if I had any notion that you did not know.'

Elizabeth glared at him. 'You are a hateful man,' she shouted as she galloped straight down the drive and made her way to the stable. Why should he try to scare her so? One minute he acted as if he was her friend, the next he said cruel lies. She did not know what the man intended to achieve, but one thing was sure, she would see her father and he would explain himself. She would not be kept in the dark any longer.

9

Jessica heard a horse gallop into the courtyard, the hooves clattering against cobblestone. She peeped around the corner of the stable door and saw Elizabeth dismount by the mounting block. The girl was obviously greatly upset by the manner of her behaviour; something had distressed her, as she stormed off into the house leaving the horse drinking at the trough. Jessica was about to run after her when she heard the other rider's horse approaching. She peeked around the door's frame and was amazed to see Mr Granger dismount and gather up both horses' reins, leading them straight toward her.

There was no other way out of the building so she merely stood still and waited for him to approach and acknowledge her.

'Good morning, ma'am,' he said, as he stopped still, waiting for her to stand forward presumably to leave the stable.

'Mr Granger, my niece appeared to be greatly upset. Are you responsible for this?' She looked at him, noticing the high colour in his cheeks.

'I should say no.' He stared blankly at her.

'Why should you? Are you to blame?' she persisted.

'Because your brother, ma'am, has withheld certain facts that he should have shared with his daughter. So in my defence I would say that he is the reason that Elizabeth is so confused about her life.' He breathed in and looked to the house. 'Ma'am,' he continued.

'Please, call me Jessica; it sounds less ancient than ma'am.' She saw a flicker of a smile on his lips and thought how handsome a man he was. Troubled was another word that she thought would describe him.

'Jessica, she has no idea what is

happening and every time I try to explain issues to her it would appear to go wrong. She has a hot spirit and will fly off when she should stay and listen. I suppose I shall have to speak to her father before she does something that she will regret, or speaks in foul temper to him. You must excuse me whilst I find that lazy stable lad and change.' He moved forwards and stepped out into the yard.

She placed her hand on his arm, feeling the strength of the man. Strength he did not achieve by being a desk-clerk as Elizabeth had so frequently described him to her. 'Better still, why don't you tell me?' She looked at him wide-eyed and what she hoped would be interpreted as deep concern for her niece's well being.

'She will listen to me . . . I can talk to her.'

He hesitated for a moment. 'Very well, but this is hardly the place.' He walked the horses into their respective stalls then yelled, 'Jimmy!' and from the end stall a fluster of hay was displaced as the stable boy awoke and scrambled to his feet. 'See to these horses and, boy, if I find you asleep again in here I shall tan your lazy hide!' Timothy shouted at the boy who was almost shaking, with what little there was of his feeble frame. Then Timothy stared at him more closely. 'Come here, lad,' he ordered. The boy moved forward, trembling. Timothy lifted his hand and the boy flinched. He touched the boy's forehead. 'Have you eaten today?' he asked.

The boy shook his head.

'See to the horses then go to the kitchen door and tell Mrs Tully that I should be obliged if she would give you a warm meal.' He turned back to face Jessica. 'There are things that will have to change around here once I am in charge.'

Jessica raised a questioning eyebrow at the man's confident remark.

'Should we take a walk . . . Jessica?'

They left the stables and Jessica

cupped her hand under his elbow steering him toward the chapel at the back of the Manor house. It was quite small but had served as a place of peace and prayer for the family for over fifty years. It was here whilst seated on a simple pew and staring up at the solitary cross that Jessica hoped the truth would be revealed. Neither saw the huddled figure on the settle behind the open door; for if they had, they would have been able to include Elizabeth personally in their conversation.

★   ★   ★

Silas was livid. He was surrounded by awkward females. Why he could not have been blessed with sons of his own he could never understand. He stared at the letter which had been intercepted in the hallway. He had returned to his room and, once dispensed with his wife's complaints over Jessica, he sat down to read it in peace. He understood Pollyanna's feelings, but turning his sister out was not even to be considered. No, once he had secured a position for her as a companion or some such for a suitable Lady he would see her rehomed. Until then she would be welcome to stay. Women caused so much trouble in his life that he shook his head as he read the letter.

My dear Jessica,

How can I begin to apologise for my behaviour toward you. I beg you to reconsider your actions. Please come home to me. I am seeking help. I have not been to that dreaded place since I behaved so badly. Jessica I love you with all my heart. Please return to me or I shall leave these shores forever. I cannot live in our beautiful home without you here to share both it and our love with me.

Everyone makes mistakes in their life, do not be as harsh as to judge me on one stupid act. I am coming back to being the man you knew and loved. Please, Jess, return to me.

If I have not received your reply by the end of next month I shall believe you cannot find it in your heart to forgive me. If you feel I am so abhorrent to you I shall have no other course but to sell our home and settle a sum on you to keep you in the style of life you are accustomed to.

Silas will be informed and asked to act on your behalf in this matter if you really desire to cease further contact with me . . .

My heart is breaking.
Yours
Herbert

'Pathetic creature!' Silas uttered the words and scrunched up the letter before hurling it at the fire. In his temper it hit the grate and rolled back out onto the carpet. So enraged was he that he stormed out of his room and headed for the library. Once ensconced with a port, he settled to waiting for Timothy to return from his morning ride. He would sort out the boy, Jessica would be found a suitable position and he would manage her funds because he would not let her grovel to such a wimp of a man as Herbert. He was, in Silas's estimation, beyond the pale.

10

Jessica was seated next to Timothy and for a minute or two they said nothing to each other. Then she patted his leg innocently and spoke. 'So, young man, tell me what it is that you have over this family. Why should you arrive here and treat this place as home? What is more, tell me, sir, why should my headstrong brother allow you to?'

'Do I behave so?' He laughed slightly nervously at her words. 'You have to realise that it is all I have ever wanted in my life. To restore my father's name and honour by reclaiming what he was never allowed to inherit. 'You may be surprised to know that my mother was a fine lady and he should have never met her. She was beautiful and beyond the reach of such a young and ambitious soldier. But . . . ' he looked down at his gloved hands.

'Are you going to tell me that this is about a tale of true love?' Jessica asked, almost incredulously.

'In a way . . . in fact, Jessica, yes it is exactly that. He should never have met this lovely lady. However, bad weather and fate played its part. The coach she was travelling on to Edinburgh was held up in a storm. They had been aiming to attend her cousin's marriage, but the journey was curtailed and the wedding party stayed at a respectable hotel in Harrogate to recover. It was whilst there she met my father, who had been recuperating from a wound gained whilst serving in France. He was young and dashing and she was greatly impressed by his heroism and the attention shown discreetly to her. They fell in love and vowed to keep in touch. Both eventually told their parents. Lady Georgina, my mother, was threatened with being thrown out of her family if she answered any of Father's letters or saw him ever again. She refused, so she was kept under house arrest and a suitor was found for her before her reputation could be tarnished in the slightest. She refused him, but her father did not listen. He also threatened my father's family with ruin. James, my father, would not take him seriously, but my maternal grandfather was not a kindly man when his will was crossed. He was determined to reap revenge when James and Georgina committed the final sin and eloped. They were wed before either of their fathers could track them down. Both were disinherited and disowned.'

'That is a very romantic story and I feel a great deal of empathy for them for I was prepared to do the same for my Herbert,' she said and then shrugged, 'but look where that has brought me.'

'Did you know love, though, Jessica?'

She laughed. 'You are wise for one so young, sir. So, explain then, if James was disinherited how can you have a claim on the estate?' Jessica asked.

'His father did what he had to to

keep the family from being ruined. Secretly, though, he kept in touch with them, funded my father to start in his own business and was delighted when they had a son. He agreed with James to let Silas inherit the estate with the condition that, so long as he did not have a son himself the estate would pass to me.'

'You are a fortunate man, Timothy, for you could have been so easily denounced. Why then do you have to marry your cousin, for you have no reason to?' Jessica saw a grin cross his face.

'She is not my cousin,' he explained simply, and now Jessica was more than intrigued.

How could Elizabeth not be, she wondered, for she had seen Pollyana throughout her confinement. 'Do explain yourself, young man, for you have my deep attention.'

'I think I have said enough to you, Jessica. I should talk to Elizabeth.' He stood up to leave.

Jessica was disappointed; she had found out half of a story but desperately wanted to know more. Calmly, she to turned around to face the doorway hoping to have one last chance to encourage Timothy to confide all in her. Both stood like statues as the door to the chapel was slowly pushed shut. It creaked on its hinges as it moved. Behind its solid form the furious figure of Elizabeth was revealed.

'You may as well continue your fanciful tale as I have heard every lie you have spun so far!' Elizabeth responded coldly.

★ ★ ★

Dora knocked on the master's bed-chamber door. There was no answer so she quickly entered and remade the bed. She went to the window and threw back the large drapes. Picking up his robe, she saw a piece of paper discarded by the fire. She picked it up and was about to throw it into the flames when she saw the fine writing and realised it was the letter which had come for Mrs Jessica earlier in the day. She had fed the poor man who had ridden all the way from London to deliver it. She could not read the words but decided it had no business being left on the floor. Surely Mrs Jessica would have disposed of it in her own room. What on earth was it doing here? Dora had one of her funny feelings about it so hid it quickly in her skirt pocket. She would have a word with Miss Elizabeth when she returned from her ride. She would be able to read it and then would know what to do, if anything. That was if the lass's mood had returned to her normal good humour and out of her current melee over Mr Granger. Dora smiled to herself. He was a fine man, just like old Mr James himself.

She shook her head. This was a becoming a right mess, someone could be hurt that was for sure, Dora thought to herself. She hoped it wasn't going to be Beth, but the girl refused to grow up and that was a necessity in life.

She left the room and nodded to herself as if agreeing with her own thoughts. Mister Timothy was just the man to help her, if only Beth would give him a chance.

11

'Elizabeth, perhaps you should sit down,' Jessica said gently, whilst the uneasy tension remained between Timothy and her niece. They seemed to be locked in a stand off as they stared at each other.

'I do not lie to you, Elizabeth. If you will only listen to me we should be able to resolve this issue.' Timothy's voice was calm, yet he was struggling to withold a lot of emotion.

'Then you are accusing my father of lying to me,' Elizabeth added.

'I would not go so far as to state that. However, they have not been open with you. Their motives are no doubt driven by what they see as your own good, yet this is not the truth. Had you been a more malleable character, you would never have questioned your duty. Then explanations would never have been sought or given.'

'So I disappoint you, what a shame.' Elizabeth's voice was terse.

'Again, Beth, you are putting words into my mouth. You have never disappointed me, Elizabeth, but you need to learn to listen and not react so quickly.' Timothy looked at Jessica.

Elizabeth saw what she thought was a flicker of disappointment as the lady wanted to stay but it was obvious that Timothy was hoping for her to volunteer to leave.

'I shall be in the morning room should you need me, Elizabeth.' She smiled at her niece and nodded to Timothy before she reluctantly left.

Timothy gestured to the pew. 'Will you sit with me, Beth? I swear before God that I will not tell you any lies.'

Reluctantly she seated herself on the pew, leaving a gap of two feet between them. She said nothing but looked up at this man who knew more about her family and her life than she did herself. It was hard for her to admit it and it hurt her deeply. Elizabeth knew she had behaved petulantly on many occasions in front of him and wondered how she could ever be her normal self around him. He stirred strange emotions within her and seemed to have the ability to wrongfoot her without apparently intending to do so.

'So what am I . . . an illegitimate child?' She held her head high.

'No, that you are not because your mother was married. Elizabeth,' he took hold of her hand, 'Pollyanna is your mother, but you were conceived by another man to your father.' He stared at her and slid a little nearer to her.

She felt slightly light-headed and the brevity of his words filtered into her thoughts. This was surely madness. 'Mother would never, ever dare to be unfaithful to Father. The notion is preposterous.' Her eyes widened as he continued his explanation.

'Your father needed a son. He had failed in the early years of the marriage to make his wife pregnant. He did not know if it was he or his wife who could

116

not propagate. Then a young man of breeding, a friend of Pollyanna from before she was wed, stayed with them. Your father knew they were close to each other and that he was a friend of the Regent himself. He allowed his wife . . . ' Timothy swallowed.

'You mean he told her to,' Elizabeth said the words hardly believing them to be true, but knowing if this actually happened, Pollyanna would never have indulged in such behaviour or any act for that matter without Silas's knowledge.

'I mean, he discovered in the following months that it was he who was infertile. This was a singular event which he hoped would provide the son he desperately wanted to secure the estate.' Timothy stroked her hand as he talked to her.

'But I am a girl . . . a woman,' Elizabeth stated obviously.

'Yes, but Silas is a clever man. Neither your mother or father would try such a perilous action more than once, and so the agreement with grandfather was changed to appease both brothers. The estate would stay in the family of Silas until I married his daughter and took my rightful place. Hence, the marriage was arranged. Your father has supported me throughout my education when my own died. He has been honourable and so shall I.' He looked at her, waiting for her response.

'But I am not my father's daughter so the agreement does not stand,' Elizabeth said whilst her mind whirled at the prospect that her father was a stranger whom she did not know. Her own 'father' was not hers.

'I cannot prove this.' Timothy shrugged his shoulders.

'Then how do you know it is true?' she asked hopefully.

'Because your father, Silas, told me it was, years ago. He was a troubled man and we are very close. The death of his brother hit both of us hard. I think he desperately wants to do what is right for the pair of us.'

'I don't understand why you would even entertain the idea of being pinned into a marriage with me when you — a man who knows the law — could have your freedom.' Elizabeth saw him smile.

'Because, Elizabeth, I have had a fairly free life. I have been to assembly rooms and met pretty ladies, and I have returned and watched you ride along the beach at full gallop. I have seen you talk to the cottagers on your father's land and have their needs met, and I have admired you from afar for years. What is more, I want to marry you.' He released her hand.

'I find all of this difficult to take on board. It is too much at once.' She fidgeted nervously. 'Answer me one question honestly before I consider your personal comments. Who, then, is my real father?'

He looked the other way but she gripped his arm. 'Timothy you have unravelled the fabric of my life, you cannot now withhold the most important piece of this jigsaw.'

'My dear Elizabeth, if I tell you this you must promise never to mention it to anyone, especially your parents Silas and Polly, for they are your loving parents and would be devastated if you treated them otherwise.'

Elizabeth said nothing but nodded her agreement and hoped she had sufficient strength of character to uphold her word.

He leaned forward and gently stroked her cheek with his hand. 'Your biological father is your Uncle Herbert, Jessica's troubled husband. But do not pre-judge him for he is a very gentle gentleman, who fell foul of the wrong sort of friends.'

Elizabeth did not know what overcame her, other than a deep need to be held which swept through her, and she fell into his arms with ease, and in a pure moment of affection felt the warmth of a caring hug.

★　★　★

Outside the chapel door Jessica stood back against the cold stone. She felt the chill wind on her cheeks as her heart, already broken, tugged one last time at the final fissure. Her love, her Herbert had loved Pollyanna. Had he married her only to be linked in some perverse way to the love of his life? Elizabeth was his child, yet she had not conceived herself. Was it a curse upon both her and Silas that they should both be barren — the final shadow of the Seabright inheritance. She staggered along the side of the chapel, leaning with her left hand against the wall of the building to keep her balance. It was only as she reached the corner of the building and looked up that she was momentarily taken out of her shocked state as she saw the flash of a red-jacketed figure run into the stable block opposite. What on earth was a soldier doing entering their home in such a clandestine fashion. She turned to run back to the chapel to fetch Timothy, her despair not forgotten but as so often of late, suspended whilst other people's problems were dealt with. Jessica had not taken but two steps when a hand grabbed her roughly from behind, holding her firmly whilst covering her mouth with his grimy hand.

'Don't squeal and I'll have no need to slit your throat, ma'am,' the voice said as she trembled with cold fear within his grip.

12

After a few seemingly timeless moments Elizabeth sat upright, dabbed the side of her eye with her kerchief then looked up somewhat embarrassed at Timothy. 'I cannot understand why you should admire me in any way. I have been rude to you in the extreme and yet you knew the details of my questionable birthright. I feel I will never live up to anyone's expectations again,' she whispered and then sniffed pitifully.

Far from gaining the sympathy or at least empathy Elizabeth thought she deserved she was surprised when he had to stifle a laugh. 'Dear Beth, I grant it that you have had a sharp shock but I think the one person who is or has to live up to your high standards, in your eyes at least, is yourself. I do not think any less of you for what was none of your doing. Besides which, you are a loved daughter, but more importantly to me, an intelligent woman and that is why I wish to share some of the outside world with you. We have both been stifled by our 'duties' — yours here, locked in your gilded cage, and me, within years of study and proving myself worthy. Now I am twenty-five I have come into funds of my own and I wish to spend some of them on travelling afar with you. Your parents are not so old that they cannot spare our company for a few years or so. I have no wish to dishonour them by turning them out of what has been their home. That I would not do, but we will raise our family there, in time. What do you say? Dare you actually venture out into that world which you have read so much about yet of which you know so little?'

His face was full of hope and happiness which Beth found very infectious. She had been disturbed by the revelation of her parentage but perhaps the opportunity to leave this place and travel might help her to put everything into a perspective which she could live with. 'Would father allow us to just leave like that?' she asked anxiously.

'Your father could not stop us for, if you are willing to accept me, we shall be man and wife and the rightful owners of the estate.' He put an arm around her shoulder and drew her in to him.

'You would be the owner, I am a woman,' Elizabeth stated bluntly.

'I cannot change the law to appease your sense of injustice but in my eyes it shall always be our home.' He kissed her forehead then slipped his body down so that he was kneeling on the stone-flagged floor in front of her. 'Will you accept me as your husband, Elizabeth?' He held her hand and looked solemnly at her as he awaited her reply.

'I hardly know you, yet I am touched by how sincere and honest you are. I would like to learn to love you first.

Could we have time together before to court . . . to . . . ' her reply was interrupted as he pulled her gently toward his body and kissed her tenderly on the lips. It was only moments before the kiss inflamed the strange emotions within her and she was lost to a place where time had no meaning and pleasure replaced the doubt. Then, he sat back on the floor and smiled warmly at her.

She cleared her throat and sat upright. 'As I was saying, time to make arrangements for our travels and plans before the wedding feast.' She looked at him and swallowed, doubting her own sanity for accepting such a stranger, for one kiss should not sway her opinion so quickly. But she knew she could be happy in this man's life, in his travels and in his arms, so what more could she ask for? The other choice to reject him would tear her family apart. Timothy, she knew now to be a fine honourable man. She even wondered if her mother was right, she was, in part, scared of the unknown, the as yet inexperienced physical side of marriage.

Timothy was about to speak. 'We shall take our time, Beth, we have our whole lives before us. Nothing can stand in our way other than our own stupidity or stubbornness.'

'It was good of you not to say 'yours'.' She looked at him as he leant back on his elbow and laughed. He was a very tactful man also.

The moment was broken in a instant as the chapel door was flung open wide, whilst a petrified Jessica was bodily hurled inside. She fell heavily against the back of a pew. Elizabeth ran to her immediately, and gathered her into her arms, but Timothy who was already on the floor, in front of the pews and out of sight of the soldier who followed her in, scuttled to the side of the chapel.

The soldier approached the two shaken women, knife in hand, and grabbed Elizabeth's arm wrenching it around and up her back. The knife pointed at her throat. 'Well, if it isn't the lady who we found in the woods — on her own indeed.'

Elizabeth swallowed hard; she saw the shadow of fear in her aunt's eyes and knew it would be a sound reflection of that displayed in her own. 'Ladies you will come with me.' He moved Elizabeth's arm so that she winced. Jessica's indecision was instantly removed as she walked slowly out of the door in front of the soldier as he ordered her to. 'To the stables as quietly as you can because my hand could slip real easy at the slightest noise; one scream could be silenced so quickly.' He chuckled quietly and pushed Elizabeth forward.

She did not dare to look around for Timothy. The man was not a coward but he was hiding. So for the first time she trusted him and left the safety of the chapel, with what calm strength she could muster believing Timothy would know what to do.

★　★　★

Dora was becoming very concerned that her mistress had not returned when she normally would. The girl's words of the previous days rankled with her. Surely, she would not take it into her head and run off. The thought alone made her feel sick to her stomach. Goodness, she thought to herself, if she knew the half of it that headstrong young woman could do anything that came into her mind. She should have been a boy. She grabbed her shawl and headed toward the kitchens. Dora had decided that she should check if her horse had been returned. Elizabeth's clothes did not seem to have been disturbed so if the girl had gone off she had done it in the clothes she was wearing. Dora prayed that her Beth was not that headstrong as to be downright stupid.

* * *

Pollyanna looked for her husband and found him asleep in his favourite chair by the library fire. The book lay open across his chest. She doubted he ever read any of them through but often was found at peace in his chair. She smiled, and stopped for a few fanciful moments of indulgence. He was, she considered a peculiar man. He was proud, but not too proud to stop his daughter being forced into a marriage she did not want. She sat in the chair opposite staring at him. Polly knew she loved him. He was strong, where Herbert had been sensitive; Silas was reliable where Herbert had been exciting, Silas was prepared to adopt and love her daughter, where Herbert could accept the pleasure of a transient act and walk away, conscience free, to marry Jessica. So who did she love the most and did she regret her one night of abandon. She looked at the books on the shelf and pictured Elizabeth as a girl reading them. Always sneaking off to this room, searching for answers to endless questions that her mother could not offer any reasonable or knowledgeable answer to, and she smiled. How blessed she had been, for a husband who had allowed her to have her own child rather than face an empty, childless life. Polly loved him, because his selfless act had told her just how much he had loved her. She left the room silently so as not to disturb him, wondering, though, how Timothy had any claim to their home when his father had been disinherited. She dismissed such thoughts as that was for Silas to deal with and was none of her business. He always did the right thing and no doubt the current confusion would be resolved very soon. Meanwhile there were the menus to agree with Cook, so she returned to the morning room and her duties.

13

Elizabeth was scared for her life. The cold air in the stable did nothing to comfort her as she and Jessica were thrown into an empty stall. The hay had been freshly turned but it was a hard, dirty landing when she hit the ground. She saw her aunt swallow hard as she fought to fight her fear. Beth had never seen her look so pale and drawn. The years, normally unseen, hidden behind the woman's smile and cheery manner, were suddenly all too apparent. To Elizabeth's horror there were two soldiers standing at the entrance blocking their escape. Where was that lazy stable boy, she wondered? Where was her Timothy, for that matter? She told herself she must stay calm. He would not desert them.

Elizabeth stood up and helped her aunt to her feet. The woman's movement was stiff and Beth suspected she had bruised her hip when she fell. Jessica, however, took hold of Elizabeth's hand and pulled her slightly behind her in a protective, even if a pointless, gesture. 'What are you doing here? What do you want?' she asked the men boldly.

The soldiers looked from one to another and grinned in an ugly and menacing fashion. 'Well perhaps you should ask your daughter, ma'am. You see we have a debt to settle with the young miss and her man friend. Did you even know she had one? They have something we need, something we lost in the woods — our weapons. Can't go back anywhere without them. Where's your fancy man, wench?' the older man asked and prodded Elizabeth's shoulder with his dirty finger.

'He is a gentleman, unlike you,' Elizabeth replied and was not surprised when her words were met with derision. She ignored the man's curses and added, 'He is still out riding. That is why this stall is empty,' Elizabeth lied as convincingly as she could.

'Well then, we'll just wait all cosy like for him to return, eh?' He winked at his friend and the other nodded. 'Best be finding something to keep us busy for a few moments.'

Jessica tightened her grip on Elizabeth as they both took a step forward inside the stall.

'The older one's yours,' said the sergeant. He grabbed Jessica and roughly threw her at the younger man who grabbed both her flailing arms and pinned her against the wooden side of the stall. Elizabeth ran at the older man, trying to kick his shins before making a break for the outside but he shoved her bodily, throwing her to the ground and was about to launch himself upon her when he let out a groan and landed heavily on the ground to one side of where she had fallen.

The other soldier swung Jessica across Timothy's path as he straightened up from hitting the sergeant. Jessica was quick, she had obviously been feigning her injury and swung a punch at the man's face splitting his lip. Elizabeth scrambled to her feet not believing her eyes as Jessica flew into a raged attack, kicking, hitting and punching the man as he crumpled to the ground, raising his arms in self defence from the torrent of wild blows.

'All right, Jessica, let him be,' Timothy said, as he wound a length of rope around the sergeant's wrists.

Jessica did not ease up. Instead, she was like a woman possessed. Timothy wrapped a strong arm around her waist and pulled her away. 'Enough!' he shouted loudly. She regained her composure, and looked at a thoroughly shocked Elizabeth.

Timothy tied up the other man and dragged both of them to an empty store room behind the kitchens where they were locked in. He quickly returned to Elizabeth and Jessica. The two dishevelled women were still standing in the stall looking at each other strangely. Despite what had happened there was something between them that had not been there before.

'Are you all right, Beth?' Jessica asked quietly.

'Yes, Aunt, are you?' It was a stilted answer and question.

'I listened to the full explanation. I know the truth, Beth,' Jessica admitted. Her hand was shaking as she held Elizabeth's.

Elizabeth cleared her throat and looked carefully at her aunt. 'It is a shock for both of us. I do not know what to say to you. It is as though we are seeing each other in a very different light.'

'Then best say nothing. In time we shall talk of Herbert but right now I would rather not.' They had not seen Timothy return; it was only when Dora arrived that they turned around and saw him approaching.

'Mercy! What in heaven's name has been going on in here?' Dora asked as she saw the dirt on the dresses of Jessica and Elizabeth.

Timothy placed an arm around Elizabeth and walked her over to the house, leaving Jessica with the maid to explain what must have looked like the scene of a fight between them.

Once the maid had been given the brief outline of the attack by their two interlopers she said shakily, 'We'll send the boy for help in the morning.' Jessica looked around as she spoke. 'Where is he?' Dora stared at her and both women shared the same awful thought and started running in and out of the stalls until one of them heard a low moan coming from the back of the tack room.

'Oh, bless his tiny frame. The basta . . . ' Dora glanced at Jessica as she had been about to swear very badly, but the woman nodded her agreement at the sentiment so Dora cradled the boy to her. He'd taken a knock to the head and lay in a huddled heap in the corner of the small room.

'Let's get him to the warmth of the kitchens then we'll see what help he needs to fix that head of his,' Jessica said anxiously. Dora nodded, but Jessica could not help but stare at her. Looking at Elizabeth's lifelong maid, she added, 'You know what happened here all those years ago, don't you? You were here before Elizabeth was born. They trust you.'

Dora hugged the boy to her tightly as she stood up. 'I'm a servant, ma'am. I see a lot and say a little. It's the way of the world. No one did anything intentionally to hurt folk. Sometimes things just happen that we wish hadn't. Once done, they can't be undone.' Dora shrugged her shoulders as much as she dare without disturbing the child in her arms.

'I thought my life was in a mess already, but now I learn this. Elizabeth has the blood of my own husband running through her veins and I could not give him a child. Have you any idea how pathetic that makes me feel?' Jessica was speaking outside of what was appropriate but Dora did not look shocked. Instead the maid gazed down at the hapless boy and then up at Jessica. 'Well this scrap of life, I'd call pathetic. He has no kin and survives on our charity. Look at him, ma'am. He was an 'accident' who was abandoned. Ask yourself, would you have denied Elizabeth her right of life? She has been raised into a fine lady, ma'am.'

Jessica thought for a moment. 'Perhaps. I should go back to him — my Herbert. I did swear to stay with him for better or worse. Hell knows, I got the worst of it in the end!' she said bitterly. 'I don't hold anything against Beth or begrudge her a good life. I just wish she had been my daughter. I like her spirit.'

Dora's face suddenly lit up. 'Now that you mention it things may not be that bad. I think I found something of yours. Don't know if you really meant it to go in the fire but I saved it just in case you'd had a change of mind.' Dora balanced the boy on her shoulder. He groaned and started to come out of the unconscious world into a confused and dopey state of reality. Dora managed to pull the letter from her pocket. 'Here, ma'am, I don't read but I recognised it as the one I'd seen in the morning. I took it from the young lad who travelled all the way from London to deliver it.'

Jessica stared wide-eyed at the crumpled letter. The hand it was written in was so familiar to her. She read the words quickly and stared at it not able to speak. Her hands were still trembling — this time with rage. 'Why didn't you give it to me straight away?'

'The master said he would whilst I saw to the messenger. I'll get the lad sorted, and ma'am, if you'd permit me to say so, I'd advise you to come in and get a tipple. You've had quite a shock here.' She moved away, but Jessica's voice stopped her.

'Where did you find this?' she asked sharply.

'It was in the master's bedchamber. It had fallen back off the grate which is why it is so charred. Didn't you leave it there?' Dora knew fine well her suspicions were correct; this woman had never seen her letter.

Jessica shook her head. 'No, it is the word from Herbert that I have been waiting for. He loves me, Dora. He is trying to recover. He has come to his senses at last. I have shocked him into saving himself!'

'I did the right thing then?' Dora asked feeling fearful as the repercussions of her actions were just becoming apparent. Jessica, the woman who had looked so defeated a few moments since, straightened her back and looked full of fight and life once more.

'Oh, I should say so. I wonder how many other letters that arrogant brother of mine has hidden from me. He manipulates people's lives in order to gain his own way. Well, he has interfered in my life for the last time. Elizabeth is my husband's daughter and that gives me claim to be a step-mother to her. I'd take a damn sight more interest in her than Pollyanna does. She is no more than a married whore!'

Dora looked shocked at the words she was hearing and placed a protective hand over the boy's ears. 'She loves Beth, ma'am. She wanted a bairn so badly — it may not have been right, but she is not a whore, ma'am,' Dora answered nervously.

'Don't worry, Dora, you have served me well and I shall protect you. I will claim to have found it. You will not be involved, but I will have my husband back. I shall never have my estate left in Silas's dirty hands. I will leave this sordid house for London within the week. You are welcome to travel with me and I shall extend the invitation to Elizabeth and Timothy.' She patted Dora on the back and walked her towards the open air outside the stable. 'Let us see to the boy, Dora. I know now who I can trust and who would play me false and that makes me feel so much better,' she said quietly and smiled. 'My life is about to begin anew.'

14

Silas almost ran to his daughter as Timothy brought her into the hall. 'Whatever happened to you? I have just been informed that we have soldiers locked up in the store room! Surely this is wrong. Why on earth would they want to come here and attack my own daughter?' His face was puce in colour. He had a riding crop in his hand and was pacing back and forth frantically. 'I'll horsewhip them to an inch of their wretched lives if this is true,' he shouted loudly and cracked the crop against a hall table. 'Did they touch you, Beth?' Silas directed the question at her, but it was Timothy who he was watching closely as if to judge his reaction.

Pollyanna appeared from the morning room rushing into the hall as if she had heard the house was on fire. The alarm clearly audible in her voice, and the animation on her face was in stark contrast to her usual pale and ineffectual manner. 'Whatever is happening here, Silas?' she asked, as she saw the state her husband was clearly in.

'Oh hush, woman! Nothing you'd understand,' he replied sharply, which caused Pollyanna to stop in her tracks and to take a step backwards until she saw the dishevelled state of her daughter. Elizabeth was standing with her arm wrapped around Timothy's waist as she leaned in to his body. His protective and reassuring arm held her firmly to him as it circled her shoulders.

'Elizabeth, my darling! What happened to you? Are you hurt?' So great was her mother's concern that she ignored her husband's order and ran to her daughter's side.

'No, Mother, I'm not really hurt, but we are both badly shaken. These horrid men threw myself and Aunt Jessica into a stall in the stables. They were soldiers — truly horrid men.' She glanced up and looked at Timothy who was still staring at Silas. 'Timothy came and rescued us.'

'Pollyanna, you take Elizabeth to her room and I'll send her maid up with warm water to wash in and a comforting hot chocolate to soothe her.' He patted Elizabeth on the shoulder and looked into her eyes. 'I need to speak with your father. We have things to arrange. Those men, I know now are deserters. They will be flogged at the barracks, then tried, hung or transported. For certain they will never cross your path again.' He smiled at her as Pollyanna wrapped a loving arm around her shoulders and walked her toward the stairs.

Elizabeth stopped on the first stair and looked from her mother to her father and then to Timothy. 'Where is Jessica, Timothy? Surely she should have come in from the cold by now.'

Timothy looked back to the door as Jessica appeared.

'Thank you, Elizabeth, for having the courtesy and care enough to ask after my well-being.' Jessica stood in the open doorway to the manor house. Her voice was calm, yet unnervingly cold.

Silas stepped toward her, 'My dear Jess . . . ' he began to speak and feign gestures of concern.

'Take one more step toward me, sir, and you shall need that crop to beat me off!' Both of her hands were clenched into fists at her side.

'I am shocked by your language, Jessica. Have you had some kind of fit that you would speak to me in such a fashion?' He looked irate but, as Jessica looked directly at him she slipped her fingers inside one of her sleeves and slowly pulled out the neatly folded letter from Herbert. At first Silas could not make out what it was but then as she unfolded it Elizabeth and Timothy both saw him swallow hard. Neither knew what it was but they were in no doubt as to the importance of the crumpled piece of parchment.

'Now, Jessica, you don't need to jump to any conclusions here. I was thinking of your best interest. That man is a user of the devil's substance. He has cast too many shadows over this family's good name for too long. You must listen to me now . . . ' He turned to face Pollyanna who had no way of knowing what was happening around her; her face looked vacant almost as her thoughts were obviously racing to try to keep up with events unfolding before her. 'Did you meddle with my things, woman? Did you go snooping in my room and decide to intervene in order to displace her once more? Answer me, did you give her it?' he asked accusingly at Pollyanna who stared blankly back, speechless, at his second outburst at her in as many minutes.

She cleared her throat then whispered, as if this would diffuse his temper, 'No . . . I did nothing wrong, Silas.'

As Pollyanna began to speak, Jessica's vicious laugh stopped her. Elizabeth held her mother's hand firmly. Whatever she had done in the past this lady was her mother and Beth understood how fragile a creature she could be.

'Aunt Jessica, please don't,' Elizabeth looked at her aunt pleadingly as she spoke, 'not here, not like this . . . ' Beth did not even glance at her father; she was ignoring his presence, not wanting to acknowledge this unveiled side to his character. Timothy backed up her words and sentiment as he walked over to her aunt's side.

'Jessica, let me take you into the morning room and there we can talk things through. This is not the correct forum to discuss personal grievances. Emotions are running too high. When you have had a drink, and we are calm once more, then you should have the comfort of a soothing bath before retiring a while.' He cupped her elbow with his hand, gently leading her across the hall.

Silas, still in a mighty fluster, blurted out at them, 'Yes, emotions are high. Tell me, sir, am I in my own home or the local asylum? Has everyone here gone completely mad?' He slapped his hands to his side apparently forgetting that he held a riding crop. He winced as it smacked against his leg.

'Sir, you shall calm yourself also. If you go into the library and have a glass of port then I shall join you shortly!' Timothy spoke as if giving the man an order.

'How dare you! I have welcomed you into my home, treated you as my very own son and you humiliate me so in front of my own daughter.' Silas was almost trembling with indignation and rage.

'But he hasn't insulted you in front of your own daughter has he, Silas?' Jessica said sharply and stared straight into her brother's face. Her words were followed by an uneasy silence as it was obvious from both Silas's and Pollyanna's faces they understood her meaning only too well.

'Come, Jessica.' Timothy led her away quickly, closing the morning room doors behind them.

The crop slipped through Silas's fingers and dropped to the floor, his hand hanging limply. He turned and looked at Elizabeth.

Pollyanna almost buckled at the knees but Elizabeth shook her arm to bring her back to her senses. 'We should go upstairs, Mama,' she said quickly.

'Once she is clean, Pollyanna, I wish to see her in the library. I want a full account of what has happened here,' Silas said as he walked to the library, his head lower than his normal proud pose.

Pollyanna was watching her husband from an elevated position on the stairs. 'Yes, however, I shall see she is well first, my dear.' With that calm comment she turned her back on her husband and, with her daughter's hand in her own, they climbed up the stairs together.

Once on the upper landing she looked at Elizabeth with moist eyes. 'We need to talk, my dear child.'

'Mama, I shall not judge you. I don't fully understand matters but you are my mother. I respect that. I just don't know . . . '

Pollyanna patted her daughter's hand and led her to her bedchamber door. 'There are things that I should have explained before. Things that are not easy to admit, yet they are worse for being hidden. Now is the time that I speak out. All I ask is that you listen and try to understand.'

15

Jessica swung around once inside the room and pointed a finger at Timothy who stood solidly between her and the door.

'You should have let me have it out with him. I would have put him in his place once and for all and, as for those two creatures in the store room, how in blaze, name did such people come to cross Beth's path?' She placed both her hands on her hips and looked at him defiantly, face flushed.

'You know, I believe that I stopped you for your own safety also. You are in your brother's house and he is a vexed man at the moment. Let me deal with him because he dare not cross my authority now. Remember that he has acted in the past for the best for both of our futures, even if there has been more than a little self interest beneath the veneer he shows to his family.' He half smiled at her. 'As to the other issue; that is a more complex story. Sit with me and I shall explain all.'

★ ★ ★

There was a very uneasy silence as mother and daughter stared at each other, not quite knowing where to begin.

'Elizabeth, I take it you have been told by Jessica the truth of your parentage. You shall have to forgive my emotions as I was not aware that she knew such things. Obviously, her drug-addicted husband had a loose mouth when he succumbed to his weakness.' Pollyanna lifted her chin as she was prone to do when voicing an opinion which set someone low.

'Mama, you are mistaken. It was Timothy who explained all to me.' Elizabeth saw her mother pale again.

'Am I the talk of the region then?' Her mama's eyes were wide. Such talk would send her into a deep depression of the spirit, Beth realised, because to her mother reputation and appearance were everything.

The door opened as Elizabeth replied, 'No, of course not, but Father explained the honest truth to him. Timothy knew more about me than I did myself.' Elizabeth stared at her father as she spoke.

'I didn't expect him to blabber it around the whole family.' Silas's appearance almost sent Pollyanna into tears. However, she seemed to be fighting the impulse as she swallowed and stared at him. 'Elizabeth, you are too young to understand these things.' He entered the room and walked over to the window near which Pollyanna was seated.

'No, I'm not! That is the problem, Father, you have looked upon me as a child, then without the turn of a hair you announce I am to marry a man I do not know and to obey your wishes, without even knowing who I am or what you stand to lose if I should not comply. Is that fair, Father?' She was standing in the middle of the room staring at his back.

He turned around and Beth could see the anguish in his face. 'I love you as my daughter. Timothy is as close to me as a son — adopted, yes. I could not wish a better match for you than he. Yes, I admit at first all I could see was that I could lose my beautiful home if I didn't produce an heir. But then I had to know if it was me who . . . ,' he swallowed hard, 'could not bear fruit, or was it your mother. There was only one way to find that out and as she already had a flame burning for Herbert . . . ' His words were interrupted by a sharp gasp from Pollyanna.

'How can you say such a thing, Silas?' Pollyanna began to protest.

'Easily, Polly, for it is the honest truth. I saw the way you smiled coyly at him when he stayed. The way you flushed slightly when he turned the sheets of music for you when you played and how your eyes softened whenever he entered a room. Oh, if only woman you had done the same with me.' He spoke softly, and Elizabeth's embarrassment was replaced with pity for both of them because it appeared they had lived out a lie. Their marriage was not a fulfilled one. Companionship and love were two very different bedfellows.

'Jessica wanted to understand what the shadow was that hung over our family. It had seemingly given Mr Granger a power over us all that we did not understand.'

'She always was a curious creature.' Her father stared at Elizabeth before continuing, 'He was still prepared to marry you, Beth; even though he knew the truth. I saw no need to tell you. I was frightened that you would reject not him, but me. I am your father!' He almost shouted the last words.

'You always will be, as Mother is my mama. I hardly know Uncle Herbert.' Elizabeth was surprised when her father hugged her tightly. 'Oh, Beth, I free you from your obligation. We shall move if he wills it. I will not force you into a loveless marriage.'

'Neither did you force me!' Pollyanna was on her feet. 'Is that what you thought?'

Silas released Elizabeth and stared at his wife. 'Have you not wished you had married Herbert and not me?'

'Silas, I knew you were a proud man but I have never taken you to be a blind one until now.' She stood in front of her husband. 'I had a girlish moment of imagining Herbert, a dashing, lively cad as a fine husband. I slept with him because I desperately wanted a child and thought that was why you had agreed, but I would never have swapped my life with you for one such as him. It is you that I have always loved, Silas — always.' She stood, not moving as if bracing herself for his rejection. Instead he held her in his arms and kissed her tenderly on her cheek.

Elizabeth had no doubt that they were indeed in love, and wondered if she and Timothy could agree to be more open with each other from the onset as words left unspoken seemed to take on a power all of their own.

When her parents both looked at her, she was smiling broadly at them. 'All these years and I have never seen you two hug one another in such a fashion,' she laughed as they both coloured.

'What do we do now?' Pollyanna asked, and Silas stepped back.

'I have apologies to make to my sister. I don't know if she will ever forgive me but I acted, at least in regard to the letter, in her best interest — or so I thought.' He shrugged. 'I suppose there is no time like the present.' He walked toward the door. 'I'll speak to Timothy and explain he can claim the house, I shall not stand in his way. It would be folly to anyway — he knows the law.'

'You'll do no such thing, Father.' She saw him face her, not at all pleased to be talked to in such a way yet, still in a humble frame of mind, he did not shout.

'It will be better coming from me, Elizabeth,' he tried to explain gently.

'We have already spoken. We need some time to know one another properly. We shall have a courtship period whilst we make arrangements.' Elizabeth smiled broadly as both of her parents looked at each other.

'Arrangements?' her father repeated, questioning her meaning.

'Yes, we have decided that once we are married we shall like to travel before we settle here; if that meets with your approval, Father?' She saw humour and relief flood across his face.

'It does, and I am grateful that you had the manners to ask, if not the necessity. But tell me, Elizabeth, were you toying with us, pretending not to want to marry in the first place?'

She openly laughed because she had not been accused of toying with people before, unlike her accusations to Timothy. 'No, Father, I just needed time to meet him properly.'

'And somehow your meeting with

those low-lives has speeded this process up?' he asked incredulously.

'Yes, in a manner of speaking, but I would ask you not to reward them for it — they are wicked men.' Her serious manner made him pat her shoulder gently.

'They will be punished, Beth. Now I must face your aunt and take whatever she intends to mete out to me. Pray for my soul,' he said and winked as he left the room.

She looked at her mother who was still flushed from the embrace. 'I need to wash and clean. Have we said enough, Mama, or do you still wish to talk?'

Pollyanna smiled. 'Enough said, I think. Now, you remove those dirty garments and I'll chase up that lazy maid of yours. What can she be doing?' Pollyanna's manner returned to normal whilst her daughter pondered what Dora could be doing.

'Mama, I'll chase up Dora. Perhaps you should wait for Father to emerge from Jessica's onslaught. I think he will need you.' As the last words left her lips Elizabeth saw her mother's eyes glisten; she knew instantly this woman loved her father with all her heart.

'Yes, dear, you're quite right. However, you give that woman a piece of your mind.' She left and, as soon as she had gone out of sight, Elizabeth flew down the servants' stairs to the kitchens, hoping Dora would be there.

16

Events had overtaken Elizabeth at such a pace that she had not given a thought about the whereabouts of Dora. Why hadn't she come back in after them — or at least appeared from the servants' hallway? It was too worrying.

Mrs Tully looked shocked when Elizabeth was seen running into the kitchens.

'Whatever is the matter, Miss Elizabeth?' she asked, as she replaced a heavy kettle onto the stone slab by the huge open range.

'Where's Dora?' she asked hurriedly. 'I haven't seen her.' Elizabeth did not receive an answer to her question from Mrs Tully because she heard Dora call her from along the corridor.

'I'm in here with the young lad,' the voice continued, so Elizabeth followed it to its source.

The open door to the little room led to one of the milkmaid's rooms but the tiny figure on the bed was not that of a young girl, it was the stable lad. His face looked bruised but his eyes were half open and swollen. As Elizabeth peered down on him, it was as if he suddenly realised who was standing there and tried to sit up like he wished he could run away. It was then she realised that it was his reaction to flee from those in the house. That was the reason why she knew so little about him.

'Dora, is he badly hurt?' she asked and saw to her relief that Dora did not have fears for his recovery.

'No, the little scrap'll have a bad head for quite a time but he won't be permanently damaged.' Dora patted his arm and told him to lie down again. 'Sorry, I haven't brought up your water, miss. I'll do it now he's settled. He don't ever speak, Miss Beth, but he works so hard for his keep.' Dora got to her feet from the small three legged stool she had been perched on.

'Don't worry about the water, Dora. I'd rather you warmed a tub for him. Place it by the kitchen stove and let him have a proper wash. Then use one of Father's older shirts for a nightshirt for him and have Jenkins fetch down a wool-filled mattress from the upstairs store, also clean sheets, blankets and a fresh pillow. Whilst he sees to that you can prepare a fire in the small grate in the room and Cook will make him a hot chocolate drink, served with some fine meat from yesterday's roast and some warm vegetables.' Elizabeth saw the fear in the child's eyes replaced with a stunned disbelief at her orders.

'Well now, who's a lucky lad then?' Dora said softly, as she smiled happily at Elizabeth and left the room.

'Thank you, ma'am,' he muttered quietly.

'So you do have a voice then. Why haven't you used it before?' she asked as she sat on the little stool by the narrow bed.

'Ain't no-one ever listened unless I got hit for the insolence,' he remarked and squinted as his head obviously hurt so.

'You sleep now and when you bathe, do so knowing that your life is going to be a whole lot broader and richer than it was before.' Beth saw a smile cross his face.

'I ain't ever slept on a proper bed before.' He wriggled a little as if he was on the softest bed ever made.

Elizabeth looked at the rickety cot, straw leaking out of one corner of the mattress he was lying on. 'Well you wait till you've slept on the wool filled one and then you'll know what a real bed feels like.' She smiled at him. 'Sleep well,' she said as she closed the door behind her.

Timothy was standing leaning against the frame. 'Have you collected a pet or are you thinking of adopting him?' He raised an eyebrow at her which told her he was not serious.

'I'm feeding him up. It struck me that

when we travel another pair of hands might come in handy.' She looked at him sheepishly.

'We'll see,' he replied.

'I haven't had time to wash and make myself presentable. So much has happened.' She looked up into his eyes as he stood before her.

'Neither have I. However, your aunt no longer has homicide on her mind. Just a good tongue lashing will appease her wronged feelings I suspect.'

He placed and arm around her waist and pulled her to him. She pre-empted his next move and kissed him full on the mouth. Her emotions welled inside her tired body. Beth knew she could easily fall in love with this man — she suspected she already had.

'Should I come back later, miss?' Dora asked, with a slightly reproachful note in her voice.

Timothy stepped back and grinned widely at Elizabeth's flustered face.

'I shall leave you to the good care of your maid, Beth, and shall see you at dinner when we are both fully refreshed.' He accentuated a bow and walked past them towards the main house.

'Miss Elizabeth! Whatever next! I never thought to see you skulking in the shadows doing such things!' Dora rebuked her, but Elizabeth merely laughed.

'I'll see you in my room when you're done here. However, I shall tell you what is going to be next, Dora.' Elizabeth saw that her maid was full of anticipation. 'The wedding will be next. I am going to honour my father's wishes and do my duty.'

'Praise the Lord!' said Dora.

Although both knew it was nothing to do with duty or her father's wishes, she had fallen in love. Elizabeth felt so happy that she could not hide her joy. 'We will marry in time, that is, and then there'll be no need for any more shadows. Will there?'

Elizabeth saw the look of approval on Dora's face. 'Best make it sooner then, after what I just saw, miss,' Dora muttered, but Elizabeth did not acknowledge her comments, because it was no one else's business what they did other than hers and Timothy's, and that would be the way their future was going be made.

THE END

We do hope that you have enjoyed reading this large print book.

Did you know that all of our titles are available for purchase?

We publish a wide range of high quality large print books including:
Romances, Mysteries, Classics
General Fiction
Non Fiction and Westerns

Special interest titles available in large print are:
The Little Oxford Dictionary
Music Book, Song Book
Hymn Book, Service Book

Also available from us courtesy of Oxford University Press:
Young Readers' Dictionary
(large print edition)
Young Readers' Thesaurus
(large print edition)

For further information or a free brochure, please contact us at:
Ulverscroft Large Print Books Ltd.,
The Green, Bradgate Road, Anstey,
Leicester, LE7 7FU, England.
Tel: (00 44) **0116 236 4325**
Fax: (00 44) **0116 234 0205**

Other titles in the
Linford Romance Library:

SO NEAR TO LOVE

Gillian Kaye

Despite Emma's dislike of Mr Peirstone, schoolmaster in Ellerdale, she is forced to go to School House to look after his children. There she meets his son, Adam, and falls in love. But Adam's circumstances don't allow for marriage. Then Mr Peirstone dies unexpectedly and Emma goes to work for Dr Redman and his wife, Amy, in Ravendale. The doctor schemes to matchmake Emma and Adam . . . but can there ever be a happy ending for the young couple?